Haven is a hero. He was born to hunt and kill supernatural creatures, which is exactly what he's done for hundreds of years.

Until he couldn't anymore.

The conclave is giving him one last chance to prove to them that they can trust him. They send him to kill a leshy who kidnaps children and kills their parents.

Or at least, that's what Haven is told.

Dimitri saves abused children. He kills their parents and finds them new families, and he's not planning on stopping, not even when the conclave sends yet another hero after him.

But this hero is different.

Haven listens to Dimitri, which is a first for the conclave. Unfortunately for both of them, the conclave won't listen to reason, and once they're on the run, they can only rely on each other, especially after Dimitri is wounded. Haven steps up as his protector, but they both know it can't last. A hero and a supernatural creature are too different to fall in love, and now that he's realized how wrong he was, Haven needs to find his way to redemption.

Can Dimitri really trust Haven with his life? And just as important—can he trust him with his heart?

Like Choices
Copyright © 2020 Catherine Lievens
ISBN: 978-1-4874-3065-8
Cover art by Angela Waters

Published by eXtasy Books Inc or
Devine Destinies, an imprint of eXtasy Books Inc

Look for us online at:
www.eXtasybooks.com or www.devinedestinies.com

LIKE CHOICES
VIKINGS BOOK 3

BY

CATHERINE LIEVENS

CHAPTER ONE

The sounds around Haven were familiar, as were the sights. He'd been back at the conclave building where he spent most of his time for weeks, but he was still having trouble getting used to it again. He didn't know why. What had happened shouldn't have changed the way he thought, the way he obeyed the conclave.

It had.

He didn't want to think about Thor and Cecil. What had happened with them had been a fluke. Haven should have killed both of them, since they were supernatural creatures and it was his job as a hero, yet he'd let them leave. He'd even allowed Thor to give him his phone number. He didn't know why. It had been a spur of the moment decision, and he would never use it. He would never *allow* himself to use it. He might be curious about Thor and Cecil and their world, but he knew his place in the world.

He was a hero, and he killed supernatural creatures like Thor and Cecil.

He hit the punching ball again, then again. He was sweating, but the physical labor wasn't helping him as much as usual. He still needed to do it, but he wished it would stop the thoughts about what had happened and what he'd done — or rather, hadn't done.

He hadn't done his job. He was a hero. He'd been born to hunt and kill supernatural creatures. Why hadn't he been able to kill Thor and Cecil, then? Why hadn't he been able to obey his orders and rid the world of the plague they represented?

1

But Thor and Cecil weren't a plague, were they? They hadn't done anything wrong.

He snorted and hit the punching ball again.

Cecil hadn't done anything. He had a shitty brother, but that was it. Thor, on the other hand, was a professional assassin. Haven knew enough about him to be sure of that. He should have killed him, but he hadn't been able to. He'd allowed Thor and Cecil to convince him the best thing to do was to let them go, and now here he was. He was lucky he hadn't been terminated as a hero. That was what happened to heroes when they went rogue and worked against orders.

But supernatural creatures were a threat to humans. There were a few exceptions, like Cecil, but they were just that—exceptions. There could be no other reason for his behavior. Haven had been a hero long enough to know that most supernatural creatures were evil.

His phone rang on the bench, and he froze. Only two people called him, and one of them was out on a mission.

That left the person who gave him orders.

He looked at the phone as if it was about to bite him. It just might. He knew he'd been lucky the conclave had allowed him to live and to continue being a hero. He wouldn't be lucky the next time.

That meant that next time, he had to kill whoever he was sent to kill. He couldn't allow his feelings and his thoughts to come between him and the creature he was sent after.

He sucked in a breath and stopped hitting the punching ball. He moved to the phone quickly, knowing Marsha didn't appreciate having to wait, especially when he wasn't on a job.

"Yes?"

"Haven. In my office. Now."

She hung up, leaving Haven to look at his phone screen until it went dark.

It was Marsha's usual behavior, so Haven wasn't overly

worried. She wasn't one for hellos and goodbyes. She didn't have a lot of free time, and she tended to use as few words as possible. It made her sound curt and hard, but that wasn't a problem. They weren't friends. She was his boss, and as such, he didn't expect to be coddled.

He took the quickest shower he could — Marsha wanted to see him right away, but she wouldn't appreciate it if he dripped sweat all over her office — and headed over to her office. Her secretary waved him in, and Haven knew he was late. Maybe he shouldn't have washed the sweat off after all if Marsha was already waiting for him.

He quickly knocked on the door, then opened it. Marsha was behind her desk, working on something, and she waved at him without looking at him. He stayed silent, letting her finish whatever she was doing. She would talk when she was ready to talk, and not one second sooner.

He stood there, waiting until she put down her pen and looked at him. "How are you feeling?" she asked.

She wasn't one to ask how one was feeling, either, so Haven knew there was something there. "I'm fine."

"Are you sure?"

"I'm sure. What happened was a fluke. I had to take care of one of those creatures, and I allowed the other two to slip away. It won't happen again." He hadn't told the conclave the truth, and he wasn't planning to. He'd come up with an excuse, and since there had been a body, it had worked. It wouldn't work a second time, though, and he had to be careful.

Marsha nodded. "Good, because I have another job for you." She paused, hesitating.

Haven held his breath. She didn't usually behave like this — hesitant and unsure.

They weren't friends, but they'd worked together for decades. They knew each other well, probably as well as anyone could know someone in their line of work. They weren't close, but Marsha was the closest person he had to a friend except for Percival. Haven knew it was hard for her to juggle those opposing aspects of their relationship. Right now, though, she was his boss, and all signs of friendship were gone.

"This is your chance at redemption. There's a supernatural creature kidnapping children and tearing apart their parents."

Haven sucked in a breath. This was why he'd agreed to be a hero. Not everyone who was born with the mark wanted to do the job, but he had. He'd wanted to protect humanity, even though he wasn't part of it anymore. He hadn't been in a long time.

Still, human beings were his people, and he would do everything he could to make sure they were safe. "Where?"

Marsha raised a folder from the desk. "All the information is here. Take a moment to read it over, then head out. I don't have to tell you we need this creature apprehended as soon as possible." She paused. "This is your last chance. If something happens, if you don't get rid of the creature . . ."

She didn't have to explain for Haven to know. If he didn't do his job, he wouldn't be a hero, and the conclave would have no need for him. They would get rid of him just like they got rid of supernatural creatures. They would kill him, and they wouldn't have one second of hesitation or regret.

He nodded curtly. "I'll take care of it."

"See that you do. I don't know what happened to you, but I don't want it to happen again. I know you can do this. You've been doing it for hundreds of years. Don't disappoint me."

"I won't." Because something worse than disappointing Marsha would happen if he didn't kill the creature.

When he left the office, he was half convinced that killing the creature was the right thing to do. His problem was that the other half of him wasn't as convinced.

With Thor and Cecil, he'd been able to see that not all supernatural creatures were bad. It wasn't black and white, and he wasn't sure what to do now. He didn't want to hurt and kill supernatural creatures without investigating and making sure they were guilty, and he wasn't sure he could trust the conclave when it came to that. He had a file, and he would read it, but he already knew how the conclave worked.

They wanted him to kill this creature, and they wanted him to do it without asking questions.

He didn't know if he could do that, not anymore.

Dimitri watched the house, doing his best to ignore the screams coming from inside. He wanted to intervene. He wanted to see the child. He had to wait, though. One wrong move and the human would escape, and Dimitri wouldn't be able to catch him. That meant giving him the opportunity to do this again, to hurt another child, and Dimitri couldn't do that. No matter how hard it was to listen to the screams, he had to do this.

He swallowed, not looking away. Even though he couldn't intervene, the least he could do was listen to the child's pain. What was happening wasn't Dimitri's fault, but he could do something to stop it, and he wasn't.

He tightened his hands into fists, keeping his focus on the house. It would be over soon, and he was relieved. He wanted the man to pay, to hurt him as much as he hurt the child.

One of the wolves growled, and Dimitri shook his head. "Not yet," he murmured.

The wolf took a step forward, and Dimitri touched the top of his head. The wolf stopped, but Dimitri knew he wouldn't be able to keep him and the others at bay for much longer.

They were wolves, yet not. He could control them, and by

now, they'd seen enough to understand somehow what was going on. They might not think like human beings, but they knew a pup was being hurt, and they wanted to save the child.

Maybe it was time for Dimitri to move on and use another pack. This one was becoming too human, even though they were wolves, and he didn't want to change them. He'd already done enough of that.

They continued watching and waiting until the house fell silent. The only thing Dimitri could hear now was the TV blaring, and he knew it was time. He peered down at the wolf, who looked up at him, and he nodded.

Then he took his hand away.

He and the pack moved together. Dimitri wasn't a wolf, but he was a leshy, and they were one. He controlled the wolves, but he didn't need to anymore. They knew what he wanted, and they wanted it as much as him. By talking to them as much as he had, by explaining why he wanted them to kill human beings, he'd pushed his conscience into them. Now, they knew what to do without him having to say anything.

They let Dimitri open the door. That was one thing they couldn't do, and Dimitri was relieved. He didn't think they would continue killing if he wasn't there, but he couldn't take the risk. He didn't want any of them to be killed because of what they were doing. The situation was already bad enough as it was, but he couldn't back down, and he knew the wolves wouldn't, either. They might be wolves, but they still understood they had to protect puppies.

Dimitri slipped inside the house. The wolves were right behind him, and he allowed them to move freely to find the man who'd been abusing the child. Dimitri already knew where the child's bedroom was, and he headed straight there. The wolves went the other way, lethally silent. Dimitri had to get to the child, to protect him from what was about to happen in the other room.

He wasn't fast enough.

When he opened the bedroom door, he couldn't see anything, not at first. Then, he noticed a bundle of clothes and a trembling child pressed in the space between an unmade bed and the wall. The child's eyes were wide, and he looked at Dimitri as if he expected Dimitri to hurt him the way his father had.

Dimitri would never do something like that, but the child wouldn't have a reason to believe him if he'd told him. He didn't have a reason to trust him, and Dimitri had to change that. "My name is Dimitri," he said.

The child stayed silent, staring at him. Now that Dimitri's eyes were getting used to the darkness in the bedroom, he could see the bruises, the cuts on the little boy's face. He couldn't be more than seven or eight, maybe even less. The sight of what had been done to him made Dimitri want to kill someone, and just then, a scream echoed through the house. It cut off quickly. Then came the sound of a pack of wolves tearing a human apart.

Dimitri swallowed. No matter how many times it happened, it didn't become easier to hear, and he didn't want it to. He just wished he could shield the child from it.

"I'm here to take you away from your father," he explained.

The child's eyes were still wide, and he was staring at the door behind Dimitri. "What's happening to him?"

"He's paying for what he did to you. He'll never be able to touch you again. Come on. I'm taking you to a better place, a place where you'll have a real family, where you'll be happy and safe."

The child was still hesitant. "For real?"

"For real." Dimitri wished he could give the child more

7

time, that he could gain his trust, especially since he very obviously wasn't human, but they had to leave before someone
noticed what was happening. The wolves weren't discreet
when they killed, and a neighbor was bound to realize something was going on and call the police. Dimitri couldn't allow
them to intervene, not until the child was away from the
house.

He wiggled his fingers. "Come on. I promise you'll never
be hurt again. I'll make sure of it."

"Is he dead?"

This child wasn't the first one to ask Dimitri that question,
and Dimitri had understood a long time ago that the best
thing he could do was to tell the child the truth. "He is. You
heard it."

"You didn't kill him, though."

"My wolf pack did."

The child pressed his back against the wall. "Are they going to kill me, too?"

"No. They're here to save you, just like I am. You can see
them, if you want."

It worked. It usually did. Children seemed to be fascinated
by the wolves, and Dimitri had used that to his advantage
several times. He already knew one of the females was just
outside the door, waiting for them, so he stepped aside. She
moved into the room, but she didn't go toward the child, stopping at Dimitri's feet instead.

The child sucked in a breath, then wiggled his way out of
the corner where he'd been hiding. "Is it real?" he asked.

"Very much so, yes. Come on. There are more waiting for
us outside. You can meet all of them before we go to a safe
place."

"And you promise no one will hurt me ever again?"

"I promise." It was what Dimitri did.

The child came closer, and finally, Dimitri could touch him.

8

He did so, opening his arms.

The child didn't hesitate. He allowed Dimitri to take him into his arms, snuggling close. Dimitri could feel the child's bones poking through his skin, and he wanted to kill the child's father all over again. He looked at the wolf, and he knew she understood what he wanted. They always did. The wolves and Dimitri were linked by something supernatural. He didn't have to use control, though, not anymore. They knew what he was doing, and they *wanted* to help.

The wolf led the way outside the house. Dimitri could still hear the other wolves in the living room, tearing the child's father apart. He whistled, telling them he was leaving and that the human police would probably be there soon. They had to leave now.

They all left the house. Dimitri was grateful the child had buried his face against his neck so he wouldn't see the blood on the wolves' fur. He stroked a hand on the child's back, trying to soothe him. "You're safe now," he promised. He was humbled by the way the child trusted him, even though he was different and clearly not human.

He was one of the children Dimitri had saved, but there were hundreds, *thousands* more of them in the world, being hurt right at this moment. Dimitri wanted to do more, but he couldn't, so he focused on this child for now. He would have time for the others soon enough.

CHAPTER TWO

It was tempting to believe everything he was reading in the file. Haven always had, so why should this case be different?

He knew why. The last time he'd been sent to kill a supernatural creature, the creature wasn't the bad guy. The person who'd called the conclave was. Haven didn't know if that was the case now, though.

On paper, everything was clear. The leshy killed parents and took their children, who were never seen again. It was too easy to imagine what happened to them, and Haven did his best not to. He didn't work with children. He avenged them and their parents, but that was it. He wasn't sure he'd be able to help a child if he had to.

That wasn't what this was about, though. Things appeared clear, but Haven couldn't help but wonder if there was more to the situation, something that hadn't been written in the report.

There had been with Thor, and even though Haven couldn't begin to understand Thor and how he lived his life, he knew that even though Thor was a supernatural creature and a professional assassin, he had honor. He only killed people who deserved to be killed. He killed people who hurt other people, and in a way, he was more similar to Haven than Haven had ever thought they could be.

What if that was the case here?

It would be easy to ignore these feelings, and Haven wanted to. He was a hero. His job was to find supernatural creatures and get rid of them. That way, they wouldn't kill anyone else, and they wouldn't take other children like this one was.

He couldn't seem to stop thinking about what-ifs, though. What if the creature had a reason to do these things? What if he was in the right, and killing him would stop whatever he was doing to help? What if he was helping somehow, and Haven put an end to it?

He shook his head and scowled at his thoughts. He had to stop. He was a hero, and his job, the reason he was born, was to kill supernatural creatures. It didn't matter what they did — if they killed human beings or lived in peace. They shouldn't exist, and Haven had been told that for hundreds of years. He'd *believed* it for hundreds of years.

He headed toward the door, ready to leave the conclave building and head to the coordinates in the report. He had a leshy to catch and kill.

The door opened before he could reach it, and a nymph was dragged in, screaming.

Nymphs were usually peaceful, so it didn't make sense that this one was being treated this way or that she'd been brought to the conclave building. She was sobbing and wailing that she hadn't done anything wrong, and Haven found himself wanting to reach out, to help her.

That would mean both their deaths, though, and he stopped himself. He watched as the nymph was taken down to the conclave jail, and he knew what would happen to her. No matter how many times she cried and told the other heroes she hadn't done anything, she would die. The conclave had to want something from her before it happened, which was why they'd ordered her brought in, but it wouldn't last long. The nymph would be dead before Haven came back.

Was she innocent? Did the conclave have a reason to arrest and kill her?

Probably not. The conclave didn't have to have a reason. They used heroes as their military force, as their professional killers. How was Haven better than Thor when he killed people he was ordered to kill without thinking twice about it?

He shook his head. He *had* to stop thinking that way. He didn't know if dragging the nymph inside was necessary, and for whatever reason, he found himself stepping closer to one of the heroes who had brought her in. Haven knew him, even though they weren't friends. "What did she do?"

Mather shrugged. "What do you care?"

"I don't. I'm just curious."

"Killed someone."

"You saw her do it? And why did she have to be brought in?"

Mather looked away from the form he was filling out. "What do you mean?"

"How do you know she killed someone if you didn't see it happen?"

"It was in the report."

And Mather hadn't stopped to wonder if the information in the report was correct. He'd obeyed his orders, just like Haven always had.

Haven took a step back. "Of course. I was just wondering."

Mather looked at him like he was crazy, then shook his head and went back to his report.

Haven should leave. He had to get out of here before he did something even more stupid than questioning this arrest. He was lucky no one else had heard him. Mather probably wouldn't report him, but someone else might, and if that happened, it would be the end for Haven.

Being a hero was all he knew. He'd been a hero for hundreds of years, ever since the conclave had found him and told him what the birthmark on his side meant. It would never change. Haven was immortal, just like some of the creatures he had to kill. The only way to kill him was through violence, and so far, he'd been lucky. He wouldn't be as lucky if the conclave found out that he doubted them, though.

He looked down at the file he was still holding. He had a job to do, and he'd better start thinking about that instead of whether or not some of the creatures they killed were innocent. He couldn't change anything. He was a hero, and he was a killer. There was nothing else for him.

Dimitri watched the child walk away, knowing he'd done a good job once again. It was always hard to let them go, but it was the best thing he could do. Even though he wanted to keep all the children close, to make sure they were safe and happy, he couldn't. He was a rescuer, but he would suck as a father.

"He'll be fine," Clementine said. She leaned closer, and Dimitri wrapped an arm around her shoulders and squeezed. They weren't together anymore, but they were still friends, and they were close. Dimitri wasn't sure what he would have done without her and the others.

They were part of the underground group that helped the children he saved. Most of them were human, like Clementine. It wasn't a problem, though. They knew about Dimitri and what he was, and they didn't care. They only cared about the fact that he helped children, that he saved them, and it made him feel like he belonged, even though he didn't. He was so different from them, but since they didn't care, he didn't either.

As long as they found the children a good family and made sure they couldn't be found, he was happy.

Sometimes, he still wished things with Clementine had worked, but she'd needed someone she could introduce to her parents, someone she could be seen with. Dimitri was nothing like that. Anyone who saw him knew he wasn't human, and that would have been a problem to say the least.

"I wish I could do more," he murmured.

Clementine pressed her cheek against Dimitri's shoulder. "You're already doing everything you can. Without you, this child would have continued being abused. Eventually, he might have died, or he could have grown up to be like his father. You're giving him a chance, and he'll never be able to thank you enough for that."

"I don't understand why humans do this." It didn't make sense to him that they didn't take care of their children.

Children were the future of the human race, yet they were treated like garbage a lot of the time, and no one tried to help them. If it weren't for Dimitri, numerous children would have died, and others might become abusers themselves. Even if they didn't, if they grew up to be good adults, they didn't deserve to go through this. Dimitri could think of nothing worse. He was glad he could help, but there was so much more to do, and there was only one of him.

Clementine moved away. "People are starting to notice what's going on," she said.

Dimitri nodded. "I know. I'm going to have to move on soon."

"I'll miss you."

The first time he'd left, when they'd broken up, she'd been in her twenties. Now she was in her thirties, but she was just as beautiful as ever. She was married and she had two children, something Dimitri would never have been able to give her.

"I don't want you to leave," she confessed.

"I know. It's necessary, though. I can't allow heroes or the human police to find me."

She wrinkled her nose. "I've never seen one of those heroes you talk about. Are they that bad?"

"It's a good thing you haven't. You don't want to meet a hero. They are monsters who kill without thinking about what they're doing. They obey orders, and that's all there is to them." And Dimitri hoped he would never meet one again.

He knew it was a moot dream. The conclave had been after him on and off for hundreds of years, and they wouldn't stop until they had him. They didn't care that he was saving lives, saving *children*. They only cared that he was a supernatural creature who killed humans, and he had to pay for that.

He couldn't allow them to get to him, though. As much as he regretted it, it was time to move on.

He cleared his throat. "I have one more child to go to in this area. Then, I'll leave."

Clementine stared at him for a moment, then nodded. "All right. Call me when you have them, and we'll be ready."

"I will." It was the way they did things. Dimitri saved the child, made sure the parent who abused them was punished, and called Clementine. She told him where to go, and once there, she and the rest of her team met him. He didn't know who else was involved. He only knew Clementine and a few other people. That way, he wouldn't be able to give them away if he was caught by the conclave or anyone else.

"I wish I could convince you to stop doing this," Clementine said.

Dimitri shook his head. "I *can't* stop. I have to continue doing it for the children."

"I know. I'm grateful for it, and so is everyone else. I hate thinking of you putting yourself in danger, though."

"Don't worry about me." Dimitri forced himself to smile, even though he didn't feel like smiling. "They've been hunting me for hundreds of years. I won't let them stop me."

"You won't be able to save all the children," Clementine pointed out.

"It's not going to stop me from trying, though." But Dimitri had been alive long enough to know that human beings never changed.

There were always abusers, people who thought children didn't matter, who enjoyed hurting them. Dimitri abhorred that kind of person, which was why he was getting rid of them. The world was a better place without them in it, and he wished the conclave would understand that. He wished the conclave understood a lot of things, but he knew better. They'd been after him for a long time, and no matter how many times he tried to reach out and explain what he was doing, they didn't listen.

This time wouldn't be any different. They were coming, and Dimitri had to make sure he left before they arrived. His life depended on it, but more importantly, children's lives depended on it.

CHAPTER THREE

Haven had read the file. He'd read it three times.

He wasn't surprised the conclave had tried catching the leshy several times over the years. He *was* surprised to find out they been trying for *hundreds* of years — literally. Usually, they managed to catch supernatural creatures eventually. The creatures made a mistake, let down their guard, and the conclave was there to kill them. The leshy was different, though. Every time the conclave tried to catch him, he managed to escape, or he wasn't there at all when the hero arrived. Haven wasn't sure what it meant, but he was about to find out.

He'd found the leshy.

He had to be careful, because there were humans around, so he was watching the leshy from afar. The leshy was outside a house, and everything was silent. Haven wasn't sure what was going to happen, but since this leshy was apparently kidnapping children and killing their parents, he was pretty sure the next few hours would be interesting. His job wasn't to save humans, just to catch and kill supernatural creatures, but if he could save lives while he did his job, he would be more than happy to do it.

There was still a niggle of doubt in the back of his mind, but he did his best to ignore it. Whatever was going on, he couldn't allow the leshy to kidnap a child.

That was what happened, though, right in front of Haven's eyes.

Haven watched as the leshy and a pack of wolves entered the house. The screams that came next were horrifying, but

Haven waited. He didn't want to attack the leshy inside the house, and if the leshy behaved as he apparently always did, he would take the child outside. It was sad that someone had to die, but if Haven did his job right, it would be the last person who would. Once he caught the leshy, he would kill him, and everything would go back to normal.

Well, except for the child.

Eventually, the leshy came out of the house, a small child in his arm. The child's long blond hair was a stark contrast with the leshy, who was darker, except for his pale skin. Haven wished he had a photo, but he didn't. That meant that if the leshy managed to lose him, he would be hard to find a second time.

Haven had to stay close.

He waited until the leshy and the wolves moved away from the house, then he followed them. He had to stop the leshy before he hurt the child, but so far, he wasn't doing anything, so Haven waited. He wanted to be sure that when he caught the leshy, the child would be safe and he would be able to kill the creature. He could have done that right now, and the conclave wouldn't have said anything. They didn't care about humans much, not even children. Haven did, though, and this child was already going to be traumatized enough. The last thing she needed was to go through even more pain.

He had almost reached them when he heard a sound behind him. He tensed, knowing he'd made a mistake, even though he wasn't sure what that mistake was. Somehow, though, the leshy had realized what was happening, and he was behind him.

Haven slowly turned around.

It wasn't a leshy hunting him, though. It was one of the wolves, and it looked ready to tear him apart just like it and the others had done to the man inside the house.

Haven unsheathed his sword. If he was going down, he would go down fighting.

Movement around him made him realize the entire pack had surrounded him. He briefly closed his eyes, murmuring a prayer to a God people didn't believe in anymore, then opened them again to face his fate. Whatever happened, this was his destiny. It always had been.

The first wolf jumped, and Haven barely managed to escape his fangs. He moved to the side, swinging his sword and hitting the wolf in the stomach. The wolf whimpered and rolled to the ground, but Haven hadn't managed to hurt it badly. Blood dripped to the ground, but the wolf still moved toward him.

Haven readied his sword, even though he didn't want to kill animals. He knew the leshy was controlling them, and he hated it. He hated when death wasn't necessary and when innocents were killed because supernatural creatures were playing with them. The conclave had been right in this case. This leshy needed to die, and he would.

"Stop," a voice snapped.

Haven froze, and so did the wolves. All of them turned to look at the man who had spoken, and Haven recognized the leshy.

He was strange, although not as strange as some of the creatures Haven had killed before. It wasn't even the first leshy Haven killed, so he was used to the sight of him.

That didn't make it any less strange, though.

The leshy was tall, with a neatly kept beard made of grass and vines. His pale skin glowed under the weak sun that streamed between the trees, and his green eyes were wide. The red scarf around his neck was the only splash of color on him. Everything else seemed to be black or green, even his hair, which was dark green and fell over his shoulders.

Deer horns rose from his head, making him look even less

human. Haven knew the leshy wasn't human in any way. He was a humanoid creature, which made the fact that the child he'd taken seemed to trust him surprising.

Haven readied himself to attack. The leshy was still holding the child, who had buried her head against his neck. It made something in Haven stop, but he knew the girl was as easily controlled as the wolves were. The leshy was manipulating all of them, and it had to stop.

To his surprise, the leshy put the child down. Then, he placed himself in front of both the wolves and the girl. She clung to his leg, no matter how many times he tried to push her away. He never looked away from Haven, though, which made everything harder.

"You're a hero," he said, his head held high.

Haven didn't know what was happening. This creature was supposed to attack him, to try to kill him. He wasn't supposed to place himself in front of animals and a child, to try to protect them. Haven's job wasn't to hurt them but to kill him, yet he didn't seem to care. He could have used the wolves, maybe even the child, and run away while Haven was distracted. Instead, he was shielding them, and he didn't look like he was going to move anytime soon.

He was gorgeous.

Haven didn't know where that thought came from. The leshy wasn't what Haven was used to when it came to lovers, although Haven had never had many of them. The only people he had sex with were other heroes, because they were the only ones who could understand him, who didn't care that he wasn't entirely human anymore.

The leshy was different, but that didn't make him less gorgeous, and apparently, Haven's cock liked what he was seeing, too.

It wasn't the first time Haven was attracted to one of the people he was supposed to kill, but it was the first time he wasn't sure whether or not the conclave was doing the right thing, and that made everything worse. What was he supposed to do? Why was the leshy staring him down, protecting wolves he could use to distract Haven?

Haven didn't have an answer to that, and he didn't know what to do.

Dimitri was terrified, but he tried to ignore it. He had to protect the child, and if at all possible, the wolves. They hadn't done anything wrong. They'd been doing what Dimitri wanted, getting justice for the child in his arms, for the others he'd already saved. They weren't dangerous for human beings who hadn't hurt children, but Dimitri doubted the hero would understand that. He looked ready to kill everyone in the forest except for the child, and that was one thing Dimitri couldn't allow to happen.

The problem was that he wasn't a fighter. When it came to the conclave and heroes, he'd always been better at evading them. He couldn't do it in this situation. The hero was standing in front of him, a sword in his hands, surrounded by wolves. In any other circumstances, Dimitri would have been in awe of the man's courage. He knew what the man was, though, so he wasn't surprised that he was facing down a pack of wolves and a leshy without blinking.

"Give me the child," the hero said.

Dimitri blinked. That wasn't what he'd expected. "Why do you want her?"

"So you can't hurt her. You already killed her parents."

The girl clinging to Dimitri sucked in a breath. Dimitri put a hand on the top of her head and scowled at the hero. "I didn't kill her parents. I didn't do anything. The wolves did that part."

"*You* are the one controlling them. You are the one who

decided to kill her parents so you could take her away. I won't let you hurt her."

Dimitri shook his head. "You heroes always think you know everything, don't you?"

The hero glared at him. "Isn't that what just happened? You went into the house, you got your wolves to kill the girl's parents, and you took her away."

Dimitri wanted to tell him what was happening, but he doubted the hero would believe him or care about it. He was here to kill Dimitri. That was always how it went with heroes. They were sent to kill supernatural creatures because of what they were, not caring one bit about what they did or didn't do. This hero couldn't be any different. None of them were.

"I'm not giving her back," Dimitri said, standing as tall as he could.

One of the wolves took a step toward the hero, but Dimitri raised a hand. He couldn't allow his wolves to get hurt. This was why he'd been planning on leaving. He knew they would protect him to the death, and he did *not* want that. He didn't want to control them, either. He couldn't help what he was, *who* he was—a leshy, a forest spirit. That didn't make him a bad person, no matter what the conclave and the heroes thought.

"Give her to me, and no one will get hurt," the hero said.

His voice was calm, but Dimitri had no doubt he would eventually attack. They both knew what would happen. The wolves would try to protect Dimitri, and the hero would kill them. He would have to if he wanted to survive.

Dimitri had to find a way out of this situation that wouldn't shed blood, but he didn't know how. The only way to do it was to tell the hero what had happened with the child and pray he believed Dimitri, but Dimitri realized how low the chances of that happening were.

Dimitri looked down at the child, then back at the hero. "I

didn't take her away because I'm planning on doing anything to her. I took her away because her father was abusing her. That's why he's dead. Because he was hurting her."

Dimitri could tell he'd shocked the hero by the way the man was blinking at him. His focus jumped from Dimitri to the girl, then back to Dimitri. "I need to talk to her."

"You don't."

"I do. I can't trust you. I'm not sure I should believe you. I *will* believe her, though."

Dimitri looked down again. He didn't want the little girl to be even more traumatized than she already was, but he could see they were at a standoff. He couldn't leave with her until the hero allowed him to, not if he wanted to avoid bloodshed, and he wasn't about to leave her with the hero. The hero probably wouldn't hurt her since she was an innocent human being, but that didn't mean he wouldn't abandon her in the forest to try to catch Dimitri.

Dimitri swallowed and looked at the girl. "What do you think, sweetheart? You think you can tell him what your father did to you?" She turned wide eyes up to Dimitri, and Dimitri hurried to add, "You don't have to give him details, not if you don't want to or if you're not up to it. But I still need you to explain. He doesn't believe me, and we need to hurry."

The girl stared at him for a moment longer. Then, she reached for her pajama sleeve. She'd been wearing pajamas when Dimitri had entered the house, and he hadn't stopped to find her clothes. He doubted she would want anything to remind her of that place. Besides, Clementine and the others would have clothes for her, and she would be able to leave everything from her old life behind.

She raised the sleeve, exposing finger-shaped bruises around her wrist. They were of different colors, indicating that whoever had grabbed her, had done it again and again. They hadn't cared about her pain.

She stepped away from Dimitri, grabbed the bottom of her shirt, and pulled it up, too.

Even Dimitri sucked in a breath this time. He'd expected to see more bruises, and he'd seen the cigarette burns on other children, but it was always a shock. He wanted to go back to the house and kill the child's father a second time. He wanted to raise him from the dead somehow and hurt him again and again, just like he'd done to his little girl.

He forced himself to look up. He'd almost expected the hero to brush them off, but his gaze was stuck on the little girl's chest. He wasn't looking away, and he was pale, even paler than he'd been earlier. He seemed to be in shock, and Dimitri hoped that would be enough to make the hero realize he was only trying to do the right thing.

He swallowed. He had to choose his words carefully. He had to convince the hero to let him and the girl go.

"This is what I do," he said, keeping his voice soft as the girl pulled down her shirt. "I take abused children and find them a new home. I make sure their abusive parents die so they won't ever be able to get them back or hurt other children. Do you really want to kill me for that, hero?"

The hero turned his attention back to Dimitri.

Dimitri waited for him to say he didn't care and that Dimitri had to die because he was a supernatural creature.

Instead, the hero shook his head. "Why? Why would someone hurt their daughter this way?"

"You've lived as long as I have. You know this is what human beings do, what they are. They're violent, callous. Some of them don't care about anyone but themselves."

"Her father is dead?"

"Since you were watching us, you heard it. He's dead. He's never getting her back, and he'll never hurt anyone else."

Dimitri was shocked when the hero nodded. "That's good. What will you do with the girl now?"

Dimitri looked down at her again. She was clinging to his leg, and he didn't have it in him to push her away. He was the one who had rescued her from the horrific experiences she'd gone through. Of course she was clingy. "There's a group that takes care of the children I save. They're human, so you don't have to worry about them. They won't hurt her. They'll take her to a new home and a new family, and they'll make sure she has all the documents to prove she's part of that family and that she always has been. She'll be okay." Dimitri wasn't sure *he* would be, though. Even if the hero allowed him to go to Clementine, what was there to say that he would also allow him to leave?

"I want to come with you."

Dimitri blinked. "I'm sorry?"

The hero put away his sword and crossed his arms over his chest. He was more vulnerable now, and Dimitri suspected he had done it on purpose. "I want to come with you. I want to see what happens to the children."

The only answer Dimitri could give him was *yes*. The hero wouldn't allow him to live otherwise, and if there was any possibility he would be able to save other children, he had to take it. "All right."

Haven hadn't expected the leshy to agree. He was shocked when the man nodded, and they stood there, staring at each other for a bit.

Then the leshy shook himself. "We have to go now if you want to do this. The police will be here soon. They always are."

He was right. Haven might not work with humans, but he knew what they did and how they worked. They always sent the police to a crime scene, and when they realized a little girl was missing, they'd tear the woods apart to find her.

Haven was satisfied to know her father was dead. He'd always known there were evil people around. He'd grown up in a time in which it was normal to abuse your children, which was one of the reasons he was glad he would never have any. He couldn't because he'd chosen the hero path, and the transformation had changed him.

He hadn't given the abused children a second thought since he'd become a hero, and it made him feel guilty. He was a hero. He was supposed to protect humanity, and it didn't matter if it was against other humans or against supernatural creatures. But here was a leshy who shouldn't be doing this and who didn't owe anything to humans, who was saving human children and probably had been for decades, if not longer.

What was Haven supposed to do? He didn't know, and he doubted he would find out anytime soon.

He waved. "Lead the way. I don't know where we're going."

The leshy stared him for a second, then he nodded and reached down to take the child into his arms again. She went without protesting, burying her face against his neck like she had before, hooking her little hand into his beard. The leshy didn't say anything about it, just looked down and smiled at her.

Then they headed out of the forest.

Haven wasn't surprised the wolves didn't try to attack. The leshy controlled them, and he had to have told them to stay back. They walked with them until they left the forest, then they stood there, watching them. Haven could still feel them as they walked toward a car. He blinked at it, wondering if the leshy knew how to drive. Haven had never learned. He didn't have to, not when he used portals to move around the world. "Is this yours?" he asked.

The leshy looked at him and rolled his eyes. "Of course.

What do you think I do with the children? Fly them to where they have to go?"

"Not fly, no. I know your kind doesn't fly." But he'd never had to think about what a leshy would do in this kind of situation.

The leshy's expression hardened, but he didn't say anything. Instead, he put the girl in the back of the car, buckling her into a booster seat then giving her a blanket and something to drink. Then, he closed the door and turned to face Haven. "Let's get one thing clear. I could have ditched you back there in the forest. The only reason I haven't is her. I won't hesitate to leave your ass behind if you don't treat me the way I should be treated."

Haven raised his hands. "I didn't do anything."

"You did. What's that *your kind* thing?"

"You're a supernatural creature."

The leshy snorted. "So? So are you."

"I'm a hero."

"And heroes are supernatural creatures. How else could you be immortal? And don't feed me that bullshit about being chosen humans. I don't kiss the conclave's ass. I never have. If you want to talk to me, use my name. I'm Dimitri."

He looked expectantly at Haven, and even though Haven knew he shouldn't be doing this, he nodded. "Fine. Dimitri. I apologize for offending you. It wasn't my intention." And Dimitri wasn't wrong. Haven wasn't entirely human anymore. "I'm Haven."

"Of course you are. That's the perfect name for you."

Haven blinked. "I don't understand."

Dimitri gestured at Haven's body. "Tall, blond. Your *face* is enough to guess your name is Haven." He sucked in a breath. "Climb in the car. We have to go."

Haven had a lot of questions, but he could see Dimitri wouldn't answer them, so he obeyed. He climbed into the passenger seat, peeked at the girl behind him, and saw she was half-asleep. His heart hurt for her, and he was once again savagely satisfied with what had happened to her abuser.

How was Haven supposed to kill Dimitri when he was helping people, helping *children?* He didn't know. There had been nothing about this in the file he'd been given, so maybe the conclave wasn't aware of what he did, or rather, of why he did it. Haven wanted to think they would agree to let Dimitri go when they found out, but he doubted it. He'd worked for the conclave long enough. He knew how they thought, the kind of decisions they made. He was going to have to be careful, because he had no intention of killing Dimitri. Dimitri was helping people, had probably helped hundreds of children over the years. Haven couldn't kill him, not for that. Not for doing something he would be doing, too, if he'd thought about it and wasn't a hero.

They drove in silence, and Haven was relieved. He didn't know what to say. He was focused on the conclave and how he would get out of the situation he was stuck in. He couldn't kill Dimitri, but he also couldn't go back empty-handed. The conclave wanted results, and this time, they wouldn't allow anything else. They wouldn't be appeased with another supernatural being, and even if they were, Haven didn't think he had it in him to find someone else and kill them just because he couldn't kill Dimitri and had to bring back something.

No. He had to find a way to convince the conclave that Dimitri should be left alive, and he didn't know if that was possible.

They drove until they reached a small abandoned-looking house with a tilted porch and trash in the front yard. The only thing that told Haven someone was there was a soft light coming from one of the windows.

The door opened as soon as the car stopped, and a woman

stood there, watching them from the porch. Haven could see she was shocked, no doubt at his presence. He did his best to stay away from her and from everyone else, hoping they would see he wasn't dangerous, not to them. He might have been to Dimitri moments earlier, but now he knew, and he wouldn't hurt the leshy. He wouldn't allow anyone to hurt the child, either.

Dimitri took the girl from the back of the car and headed toward the woman, who was still staring at Haven with wide eyes. "He's with me. Don't worry about him," Dimitri told her.

"Who is he?"

Dimitri shook his head. "A hero. But he's not here to hurt anyone."

The woman's eyes went even wider, and she took a step back. "You have to run away. You know you can't trust heroes."

"Maybe not, but this one stopped. He listened to what I had to say. I can't trust him, but I know he won't do anything to hurt the child." Dimitri looked at Haven for a second, then turned his attention back to the woman.

They walked inside, and Haven could tell more people were in the house from the sounds. They weren't in the front room, though, and since the child wouldn't let go of Dimitri no matter how much he tried to coax her, he had to walk her wherever she was going.

He looked at Haven. "I can't allow you to meet the other people here. They're part of the group who takes care of the children and finds them a home. No one can know them, especially not you."

Haven wanted to push, but he understood. "I'll be here."

"I'll keep an eye on him," the woman said.

Dimitri looked like he wanted to protest, but instead, he nodded curtly and headed deeper into the house. The door closed behind him, leaving Haven alone with the woman. They stared at each other for a moment, and he wondered what she was going to do. It was obvious she didn't like him, and he didn't blame her, not with what he himself knew of the conclave and the other heroes. Considering how many times Dimitri had been hunted, he no doubt had strong opinions on the conclave and heroes.

The woman was pretty. She had to be in her late twenties, although Haven wasn't great at estimating age, especially now that he didn't age anymore. Her dark hair fell around her face, and her nose was slightly crooked, but it made her face more interesting rather than detracting from her beauty. She wore a black sweater and jeans, along with boots.

"He's been doing it for years, you know?" the woman said.

"I suspected it. The whole operation is too smooth for him to have started recently."

"It's what he does. He rescues people." She paused. "He rescued me almost thirty years ago. I was being abused. He took me away, and while the people helping him were different back then, he had a similar organization set up. They found me a new home, and I was able to grow up happy and safe." Her eyes shimmered with tears. "I know your job is to kill people like Dimitri. But please. He's never hurt anyone, not anyone who didn't deserve it. He's doing this for the children, and if you kill him, they will lose their champion and one of the few people who care about them and can help them."

"I'm not the one who makes decisions." But Haven didn't think he could kill Dimitri. He believed the woman, and everything she'd told him, along with what he already knew, told him a lot about the kind of person Dimitri was. He still had to kill Dimitri, though.

He couldn't.

Leaving the children behind was always hard. If Dimitri could choose, he would keep all of them, and they would live together as he raised them. He couldn't do that, though. It was dangerous, and he had to help other children. There were *always* other children.

So he said goodbye to the little girl. She clung to him some more, but the people he worked with knew what they were doing, and they distracted her enough for Dimitri to manage to slip out. He felt guilty, even knowing it was the best thing to do. If he didn't go, she would continue clinging to him, and she had to let him go and start her new life. He wouldn't be a part of it. He couldn't be a reminder of what had happened to her, what had been done to her.

He briefly closed his eyes as he left the room, then opened them again and went back to Haven and Clementine.

He was wary about what he would find when he got to them. Surprisingly, he trusted the hero with Clementine. He wasn't sure why—heroes weren't trustworthy. But this one had listened to him. He hadn't tried to kill him, not after he'd found out what had happened. He'd seemed angry on the child's behalf, and Dimitri hoped it meant he would let him go.

He snorted at himself. He'd been tangling with heroes for centuries. He knew the conclave, and they wouldn't take it well if Haven went back without Dimitri's head, or something equally horrifying. If Haven wanted to make it, if he wanted to continue being a hero and to live, he would have to show proof he had killed Dimitri.

Dimitri didn't know what would happen now. He was worried. He'd been helping children for a long time now, and he didn't want to stop. He couldn't allow the conclave to push him into doing that, but he also couldn't allow the conclave to hurt him. Who would help the children if he wasn't there anymore? Clementine and her group could do some of the things that were needed, but they weren't Dimitri. They'd never taken care of his part of the process, and he didn't want them to. They were human. They already put themselves in danger by taking the children away. He wasn't going to allow them to kill other human beings.

He didn't know if he would be allowed to do anything else, though. He would have to convince Haven that the best thing for everyone was to let him go, but he wasn't sure there was a way to make that happen, not when Haven's own life was in danger. The conclave was uncompromising. Dimitri should know, considering all the times he'd faced them.

Dimitri swallowed and joined Clementine and Haven. They were talking, but they stopped once Dimitri came into the room. Clementine strode toward him, wrapping her arms around him. "Do you need help?" she murmured. "I can help you escape through the backdoor or something. I'll even keep him distracted."

"I'll be fine," Dimitri murmured back. If he was going to die tonight, he didn't want Clementine to know about it. She'd suspect, of course, but she was also used to him disappearing when he had to. She would worry, but she'd think he'd managed to get away, and she would hope to see him in ten years, maybe fifteen. She might have forgotten all about him when the time came and he didn't come back.

He wouldn't go down without a fight, though. He never had, and the current situation wasn't any different.

He headed out after kissing Clementine's cheek, and sure enough, Haven followed him. "What's going to happen to her?" Haven asked.

Dimitri knew he was talking about the child. "She'll be taken to another town. The group already has everything in place. They know who's going to adopt her."

"How can they know those people will be better than the

child's father?"

"Because they vetted them. They know what they're doing, Haven. I've been working with them for decades."

"You can't have been working with some of them for that long. Your friend isn't much older than thirty."

That made Dimitri smile. "I'll tell her you said that, but she's thirty-five. And yes, I've been working with her for more than ten years." Dimitri would always remember meeting Clementine. It might sound strange to some people that he'd saved her when she was a child, then had a relationship with her, but it wasn't. He hadn't watched her grow up. He'd saved her, then, he'd handed her off to the group, just like he'd done tonight. He hadn't seen her again until she was almost twenty-five.

And now he didn't know if he would ever see her again.

He cleared his throat. "I know you're worried about her, and it's hard for you to trust me because I'm a supernatural creature. These people are all human, though. They know I'm not, and they don't care, not as long as I continue doing what I do. They care about the children. Unfortunately, there is no other way to save them. Most other humans don't care about them, and they don't help them as much as they should. That's where we come in. I take the children, make sure their parents won't be able to get them back, and the group finds them a new home. I will never see the little girl again, not unless she wants to be part of the group. She'll be safe, though. It'll take her time to work through what happened to her when she was a child, but she'll have therapy and a loving family. You don't have to worry about her anymore."

"I don't know if that's possible."

Dimitri understood that feeling well. He didn't want to give Haven too much information, but he also wanted Haven to see what he did. He wanted Haven to understand what would happen if he were to disappear. No more children would be rescued. They would stay in their abusers' hands, and Dimitri would lose his life.

He didn't want that to happen.

He looked at Haven as they climbed into the car. He had no idea what was next, and he realized he wasn't the one in charge. He could probably try to slip away, but Haven was a hero. He would find him again. They always did, and Dimitri had exposed himself and made himself vulnerable by bringing Haven here. Haven held all the cards, and until Dimitri knew how he would play them, he couldn't decide what was next.

He swallowed. His mouth was dry as the desert, and it didn't help. "What now?" he asked.

Haven didn't know how to answer. He knew what the conclave expected from him, and he knew what he wanted to do. He had no idea how to reconcile those two things, though.

He swallowed and looked at Dimitri. "The conclave sent me to kill you."

Dimitri didn't look surprised. "They've been trying to kill me for centuries. I'm not surprised they're still after me. I *am* surprised at how easily you found me, though."

Haven shrugged one shoulder. "I'm good at what I do." And didn't that make him feel bad? Now that he thought about it, he couldn't help but wonder about the supernatural creatures he'd killed. Had they deserved it? Had they actually hurt human beings? Or had the conclave just wanted them out of the way? The conclave thought supernatural creatures didn't deserve to live, that they had no place on this earth, but Haven had started to wonder, and now, he couldn't help but think they were wrong. Surely, someone like Dimitri, who was doing his best to help people, to help *children*, didn't deserve any of this.

Haven wanted to believe the conclave would agree with him, but he didn't know if that was the case.

"I don't care what the conclave wants," Dimitri continued. "I already know. They've been trying to kill me for a while, and they haven't succeeded yet. I want to know what *you* are going to do. You're not the conclave, even though you're a hero. You might think you don't have a choice, but you have a say in what happens next."

Haven wasn't sure about that. He wanted to do his job. The conclave and the other heroes were the only things he'd known for hundreds of years. He didn't know what he would do if he lost them. They were his family, even though some days, he wasn't happy about it.

Could he really kill Dimitri to make that happen, though? Would he be able to live with himself if he hurt a man who was helping children?

He rubbed his face, unsure of what was to come. He still didn't know how to answer Dimitri's question. He wanted to believe the conclave wouldn't be as black and white as Dimitri thought it was, but how could he? The last time he'd allowed a supernatural creature to live, the conclave and Marsha had made it obvious that they wouldn't be as nice if it happened again. If Haven didn't kill Dimitri, he would be the next one on the conclave's kill list. He had to choose — his own life or Dimitri's.

He had no idea which way he would go.

He wanted to protect himself, but he couldn't do it by killing Dimitri.

"I'll call my superior. She can contact the conclave and try to convince them you're doing the right thing."

Dimitri shook his head. He looked sad, and Haven didn't like it. "They won't care. They never do. You're not the first hero to whom I've explained what I do. You *are* the first one who didn't try to kill me on sight, though."

Haven didn't like that, either. Dimitri was doing his best to help people, and this was how the conclave thanked him?

The conclave was supposed to protect humanity, but over the years, they'd become something else. Now they wanted to kill people who were different, and they used the heroes to do it. It wasn't fair, and Haven despised that he'd gone along with it for so long. He couldn't anymore, but he had to find a way out of the situation he was stuck in. He had to find a solution before something happened.

"I'll call," he repeated. It was the only thing he could think of at this moment, and while he might be able to come up with something else eventually, he doubted it.

He didn't have much of a choice. Either he killed Dimitri and regretted taking away such a bright light from the world, a man to help children, the most vulnerable of human beings, his entire life, or he allowed Dimitri to leave and lost his life in the process.

How was he supposed to make that choice?

CHAPTER FOUR

Dimitri started driving away, but he didn't know where to go. He didn't have a place to stay. Usually he stuck to the forest, sleeping and hunting with the wolves. He couldn't do that with Haven with him, and besides, he had to leave the area before the conclave sent more people after him.

Because there was no way they would listen to Haven.

Dimitri knew it was foolish even to suggest that they would let him go, but he was grateful to Haven for suggesting it. He'd thought Haven was a bloodthirsty monster, just like most of the conclave and the heroes, but instead, he'd taken the time to listen to Dimitri, and he'd seen how important Dimitri's work was. He was still going to contact the conclave, even though Dimitri could have told him it was useless, but he understood. Haven was a hero. He'd probably been a hero for decades, if not longer. The conclave was the only home he knew. He didn't want to lose it, not if there was anything he could do about it.

There wasn't, no matter what he kept telling himself.

Dimitri should run. The conclave wouldn't allow him to go, which meant Haven would have to kill him, even though he didn't want to. It was either that or for Haven to lose his life, and Dimitri wasn't stupid enough to believe Haven would sacrifice his own life for Dimitri's. No matter what he did, how many people he helped, no one would sacrifice anything for him.

He reached for Haven's arm before Haven could make the call. Haven looked at him, blinking, and Dimitri shook his

37

head. "Wait. Let's get back to the forest." Dimitri wanted his wolves with him. He *needed* them with him, to protect him. If Haven decided he was going to kill him like Dimitri thought he would, Dimitri wouldn't let him do it without fighting back. No matter how much he liked Haven, Haven was still a hero, and he was good at what he did. Dimitri would need all the help he could get, and that meant his wolves and possibly other creatures in the forest. He didn't like the thought of using them and getting them hurt or killed, but there was no other way.

Haven lowered his arm. "All right. In the forest."

So back they went. Dimitri hadn't been planning on this, but he knew better than to think he could convince Haven of anything. No. They were going to fight, and only one of them would come out of it alive. Dimitri could only hope it was him. He didn't want to die. Maybe he would manage to distract Haven with the wolves and to shift and run away. It had worked before, and it could work again.

The thought of sending Haven back to the conclave was terrifying, though. He was the first hero who'd listened to him. He was the first hero who understood, who gave Dimitri more credit than usual. He was the only one who'd seen Dimitri as a human being, someone who did good things instead of bad ones.

Dimitri didn't want him to die.

He didn't want himself to die either.

He parked the car by the forest. It wasn't his, and he knew that if he didn't use it to run away, the police would eventually find it and get it back to its rightful owner. Dimitri couldn't allow himself to have a car or anything that tied him down. He was always on the move, and that wasn't going to change anytime soon. It couldn't. The conclave was still after him, and they wouldn't stop until they got to him.

They stepped into the forest, and Dimitri instantly relaxed.

This was his home, the place where he belonged. Here, he was safe — or as safe as he could be, considering he was standing next to a hero.

Haven looked at him. "Can I call now?"

"You can. It's not going to help, though."

Haven grimaced, then took his phone out. Dimitri turned, smiling when he saw the wolves gathering around them. They didn't like Haven much, but that was mostly because of the way he'd tried to stop them earlier. Given time, they would understand Haven wasn't a bad person.

Haven grabbed Dimitri's arm, and one of the wolves growled. They all stepped closer, then Dimitri raised his free hand, shaking his head at them. "I'm fine."

"Are you sure you are? I don't like those wolves," Haven said.

Dimitri almost snorted because Haven thought he'd been talking to him. "I was reassuring them. They're no danger to me. You, on the other hand, definitely are."

"You control them," Haven said, looking around.

"I can if I want to. I'm not controlling them right now, though. They want to protect me because they love me and because I've been working with this pack for decades. They're not the original wolves, but they know me, and they treat me like one of theirs. They won't let you hurt me." *There.* Now, Haven knew what was going on, and he'd been warned.

Haven didn't look convinced, but he let Dimitri go. "Stay close by."

Dimitri wanted to ask if that was because it would be easier for Haven to kill him when the conclave ordered him to, but he didn't. Instead, he nodded, then watched as Haven dialed the number.

Both of their lives hinged on what was going to happen next, and Dimitri hated that he already knew how things would go. There was no way the conclave would allow Haven to let him go, which meant it was going to be his life or Haven's.

He didn't know who would win, but one thing he was sure of—neither of them would come out of this in one piece, be it physically or mentally.

Haven made the call. He held his breath as he waited for Marsha to answer, but when she did, he couldn't say anything for a few seconds.

"I hope you have good news," she said, not saying hello or asking how Haven was.

He swallowed and forced himself to answer. "Marsha. I have something to tell you."

There was a pause, then Marsha asked, "You didn't do it, did you?"

"I couldn't. I found out why he was killing people and taking children. He's saving them. He kills their abusive parents and gives them a better life."

"Your job was to kill him. It wasn't to talk to him."

"I know, but I can't kill him. He's not doing anything wrong. Hell, he's doing everything *right*. He's helping those children, and if I kill him, no one else will benefit from what he's doing." The conclave certainly wouldn't. They might have been created to protect human beings, but over the years, they'd stopped taking that part of the job seriously. Now, they were focused on dominating their world. They killed supernatural creatures, no matter what they did, because they could and because of the power it gave them.

But Haven thought the conclave could still change. He believed heroes were better than that, and that eventually, they would realize what was going on. He had to convince Marsha he was doing the right thing, though.

"I can talk to him," he continued when Marsha didn't say

anything. "I can ask him not to kill humans anymore. It might be a risk for the children, but if that's a problem, I'm sure we can find a way to solve it."

Haven was surprised when Marsha sighed. He could hear the tiredness in her voice when she answered, "I understand what you're saying. What that leshy is doing is a good thing. I can't deny that. I wish we could let him go, but you know it's not possible. He's a leshy. That means he has to die."

Haven swallowed. "He's not doing anything wrong, though. Why should we kill him for what he is, for something he never had a say in and that he can't change?"

"You know your orders. I have mine, and I need you to do this. Please, Haven. I don't want to lose you. The conclave will send someone if you don't kill the leshy, and they will send someone for both of you, not just for him. You have to obey your orders. It's the only thing that makes sense right now, and the only way you'll save yourself."

Haven disagreed. He knew he wouldn't be able to convince her, though, not when he was going against the entire conclave. "Thank you for telling me the truth," he said.

"I wish I could do more, but I can't. You don't have a choice, Haven. Either you kill him, or you end up dead with him."

She didn't say goodbye when she hung up, and Haven was grateful. He didn't want her to change. She'd always been curt but somehow caring, and she had been just now, too.

That left him with a choice to make.

He put away the phone, then looked for Dimitri.

He was still hovering close by.

Haven had half expected him to run away, especially since he'd been listening in on the conversation. It would have made sense, but instead, he remained standing, looking at Haven, and from his expression, Haven knew he was aware of what was supposed to happen next.

Haven rubbed the back of his neck. "I'm sorry I couldn't do more," he said.

"They're not okay with you leaving me be, are they?"

"My orders are to kill you. I'm sorry," Haven said again. No amount of him apologizing would change the situation, though.

Dimitri stood up straighter. "I'm sorry we're going to have to fight, because I'm not going down without trying. I won't just let you kill me."

Haven hadn't been expecting anything different from the little he knew about Dimitri. "I'll help you run away."

Dimitri blinked, and his shoulders slumped just slightly. "What are you talking about? You can't help me run away. They'll kill you."

"They'll kill me anyway."

"Because you won't kill me?"

"Because I didn't obey their orders. It's not allowed. I already did that once, and they won't let me do it twice, especially not when this mission was supposed to be my redemption."

"Yet you would still help me run?"

"I have to. I won't be able to live with myself if I don't." And if he did manage to get Dimitri away, well, he wouldn't have long to live. He knew the conclave. They wouldn't waste time. Hell, he was surprised they'd sent him in the first place, especially since it was becoming obvious they knew what Dimitri was actually doing. Marsha might not have known, but the conclave certainly had. They'd been hunting Dimitri for long enough, and Dimitri had tried to explain to the other heroes who'd found him.

"You'll be on the conclave's hit list if you do this," Dimitri pointed out.

Haven didn't want that. He didn't want to leave his home behind. The conclave and the other heroes were everything he'd known for hundreds of years, ever since he'd left his human life behind and had agreed to be trained. He was going to lose that, and the thought was terrifying. What was just as terrifying was the thought of killing an innocent man, though. Dimitri was helping people. He was helping *children*, and while Haven would never be able to have any of his own, it didn't mean he didn't want to help them.

He shook his head. "This is how things are going to go. I can't kill you. I would never forgive myself for doing it, and I can't allow that to happen. If the conclave finds me and kills me, then so be it. I've lived a long time anyway." And now that he was losing the conclave, he didn't know what else he could do. Being a hero was what he was, and that wouldn't change. He'd been a hero since he was born. He was marked as one. Leaving the conclave wouldn't change that, and he would die a hero, whether or not they liked it.

Hopefully, it wouldn't come down to that, but there was no way for him to know. He could only pray, and once again, he invoked one of the Gods people didn't pray to anymore.

Dimitri could see how torn Haven was, and he didn't like it. Even though they'd just met, he didn't want Haven to be in pain. He was doing the right thing, even though it went against everything he'd been taught and had believed for so long.

Dimitri hadn't expected this. Even though he could tell Haven was a good man by the way he'd stopped and asked questions when he'd found out about the children, he hadn't thought Haven would be ready to sacrifice his own life.

He was also grateful, though. Haven wouldn't blindly obey the conclave and the orders he'd been given. He was challenging everything he knew, probably because he could tell something was wrong. Dimitri had known for hundreds of years. That was how long he'd been fighting the conclave. It was made up of heroes who had risen through the ranks over the decades, and their immortality meant they weren't replaced. Most of them had always been small-minded, and they truly thought that only heroes and human beings were good and should be allowed to live. Some of them thought heroes were better than *anyone*, including normal humans, and Dimitri wouldn't be surprised if eventually they decided to kill humans, too. It would only be a step away from killing supernatural creatures for what they were.

But this wasn't the moment to think about that. Now was the moment to focus on Haven and what he was going to do next.

"We should get some sleep," Dimitri said without thinking.

Haven looked up at him, his gaze sharp. "I just told you I'm supposed to kill you, and you want to go to sleep?"

Dimitri shrugged. "I already know you won't kill me. You told me as much."

"I could also change my mind. I'm a hero. I'm set to lose everything I know if I don't kill you, yet you truly believe I won't, and I don't understand that."

"I do. You've had plenty of occasions to kill me. Even if you'd decided to wait until the child was gone, you still had enough opportunities, yet here I still stand, and we're talking instead of fighting and trying to kill each other. So no, I don't think you're going to kill me, and I'm tired." Dimitri was always tired after one of his raids. Seeing the children in the state they were in, having to force himself to face that situation again and again was draining, today especially so with the addition of Haven, and Dimitri couldn't wait to go to bed.

But he doubted Haven would let him go easily. Even if he wasn't planning on killing him, he seemed to have decided he wanted to save Dimitri, and that might not be the best idea. It meant spending time with him, closer than Dimitri had ever been to a hero, at least without the hero trying to kill him. He might want to trust Haven, but could he really?

"I can't allow you to leave on your own," Haven snapped, his voice stronger. "I won't kill you, but the conclave *will* send someone else. You have to be protected."

Dimitri bristled. His first instinct was to tell Haven he didn't need to be protected, that he'd been doing this for hundreds of years and he knew what he was doing. Haven wasn't wrong, though. The conclave would send someone else, and since they knew Dimitri had somehow convinced Haven to go against their orders, they would be extremely careful. They would send someone who was good at this, maybe one of the other heroes who had found Dimitri over the years. Dimitri still remembered some of those — he bore the scars they'd left on his body — and he wasn't looking forward to being found by any of them.

Still, he was puzzled by Haven's behavior. It was one thing to admit that Dimitri shouldn't be killed for what he was doing, and it was another to decide to protect him against the conclave. "You could tell them I ran away," he suggested.

Haven shook his head. "It won't work. I already did that once, and even though they believed me and allowed me to stay, it won't work a second time. Besides, I already called my superior. She knows I won't kill you."

"You should let me leave anyway. We can go our own way. I know you have to run from the conclave now, too, and it's going to be easier if we're not together."

"What happens if the other hero finds you? How will you defend yourself?"

Dimitri glared and crossed his arms over his chest. "I've defended myself for hundreds of years. I can do it again if I need to." Even though he would rather not, since he was exhausted.

Haven looked him up and down. "I'm impressed by the way you managed to deal with the conclave all those years. Still, I don't think I can let you go on your own. I would feel guilty if the hero found you and hurt you, or worse. I can't let that happen."

"Because of the children."

Haven blinked. "Because of you. I don't want you to get hurt."

That was even more confusing than the rest of the situation, and Dimitri didn't know what to do with it. He also knew he wouldn't be able to think straight until he got some sleep, though. "Fine. I'll stick with you. Where are we going? I've been sleeping in the forest, but I doubt that's what you want to do."

Haven looked lost for a second. Then, he shook his head. "We'll find a motel. I'm sure there are some close by."

Dimitri couldn't say he was sorry. He was used to sleeping in the forest, but he didn't mind comfort, even if it was only for one night. He was also yearning for a warm shower. It had been ages since he'd washed with anything more than cold water. Hopefully, there would even be soap and shampoo.

He bounced on his toes a bit, causing Haven to shake his head as he looked at him. "You look happy," Haven said.

Dimitri shook his head. "I'm not happy, per se. I'm looking forward to having a shower. I love the forest and living here, but some days, I'm also grateful for the comforts human beings invented. A warm shower is one of them. Warm food is another."

Haven nodded. "You'll have all of that. We should go. You need some sleep, and we can talk more once we're both rested."

Dimitri wasn't sure he'd be able to fall asleep in a room he shared with Haven, but he supposed he was about to find out. There was no way Haven would allow him to sleep on his own.

They headed toward the nearest small town, a different one from where they'd delivered the girl, just in case. Once they found a motel, another problem arose.

"I can't let anyone see me," Dimitri said. He might be able to pass his green hair for one of those tints some humans favored, but there was nothing he could do for his beard and horns, not unless he shifted, and he wasn't ready to show Haven that side of himself yet.

"I'll take care of it. Wait in the car. I'll get a room with two beds."

"How will you pay?" Dimitri suspected the conclave provided their heroes with everything they needed, included money, but Haven couldn't use it, not if they didn't want the conclave to find them.

"I'll use my personal funds." Haven appeared amused by Dimitri's skeptical expression. "I might be a hero, but it doesn't mean I'm an idiot."

He left the car, and Dimitri watched him go. He didn't know what would happen next, couldn't guess, and it was terrifying.

CHAPTER FIVE

When Haven woke up the next evening, it took him a moment to wrap his mind around everything that had happened. He'd tried to do that last night, too, but it had been impossible to focus with Dimitri so close to him. He'd also been hypervigilant, expecting another hero to burst into their room to kill both of them.

They were still alive, and to his own surprise, Haven had slept. Not well, but he felt better and more rested.

It was only a question of when—not if—another hero would be sent to kill Dimitri, and probably Haven now, too. Marsha had been clear, and she knew Haven hadn't killed Dimitri. That meant that someone else would, or at least, they would try.

He turned around in his bed, facing Dimitri. They'd been lucky enough to find a room with two beds, so they'd each taken one of them. Haven had had a hard time falling asleep as it was, and he could only imagine how much harder it would have been if he'd had to share a bed with Dimitri.

Dimitri was curled under the blanket, a tight ball that moved as he breathed. The blanket was pulled up to his chin, so Haven couldn't see anything but his face.

It was gorgeous.

All of Dimitri was gorgeous in an alien kind of way. He wasn't the first supernatural creature Haven found beautiful, but he was the first one that made Haven want to touch him—and not to kill him. Haven should stop thinking about how soft Dimitri's hair would feel sliding between his fingers, though.

He didn't know what exactly attracted him to the leshy. Maybe it was the way Dimitri looked, with his strange beard and horns, or maybe it was how gentle he'd been with the child and what he'd been doing for all the children he'd saved. Dimitri was a good person, even though he wasn't human, and Haven didn't understand why the conclave couldn't see that. He knew where they were coming from — over hundreds of years, they'd had to fight supernatural creatures who were hell-bent on killing the human race, on making the world a place where only they would reign. Dimitri was different, though. He didn't want anything for himself except to be left alone and saving children.

Dimitri moved, rolling to his back, dislodging the blanket from around him. It exposed his upper body, and Haven swallowed and looked away when he saw the expanse of skin.

Dimitri was pale, even paler than Haven, and that was a feat. It had to do with the kind of supernatural creature he was, and Haven would have never thought he would find it attractive. The green color also was odd, but not unpleasant. Dimitri's hair was of a dark green that reminded Haven of the forests in which he'd grown up as a child — of a different time, a time in which he'd been fully human, in which his only worries were to help his parents and keep an eye on his siblings. It had been a long time ago, and Haven wouldn't change the choice he'd made to leave all of it behind. He might wish he hadn't eventually, but he couldn't start thinking about whether or not he'd done the right thing then and since, not unless he wanted to freak out.

But he wasn't here to be reminded of the past or to stare at Dimitri's half-naked body.

If he didn't kill Dimitri, someone else would be sent to do

it. Dimitri had to leave and continue running from the conclave the way he had for centuries.

But it was a big change for Haven. He couldn't stay with the conclave if he didn't kill Dimitri, and he wouldn't be able to live with himself if he did kill him. Dimitri didn't deserve it. That was one thing Haven was sure of.

At this point, it was also obvious that the conclave wanted Dimitri dead because he was a supernatural creature and for no other reason. They didn't care how much good he did. They didn't care about anything but the fact that he wasn't human, and Haven despised that. He didn't want to do this. He wanted to be able to look at himself in the mirror in the morning, and that wouldn't happen if he killed Dimitri.

It also wouldn't happen if the conclave killed him, though.

The way Haven saw it, there were only a few ways out of the situation. Either he killed Dimitri—and he already knew he wouldn't do that—or they both went on the run. Haven might be able to convince the conclave to rethink their decision over time, but right now, they wouldn't listen. They'd expected him to fail. He'd only just now realized that, but he was sure of it, and he knew they wouldn't listen to him. There could only be one reason they'd sent him, of all people, after Dimitri. They'd wanted to test him, and he'd failed spectacularly.

He sighed.

Either way, he was going to lose a lot today. Either he lost all respect he had for himself and killed Dimitri, or he lost the only family he'd known for hundreds of years.

What mattered more for him?

When Dimitri woke up, Haven was staring at him.

It only lasted a moment, until Haven realized Dimitri was awake and looked away. Still, it was enough to make something flutter in Dimitri's stomach, and it was the worst moment for something like that to happen. Yes, Dimitri liked Haven, and he was impressed that the man was ready to do the right thing rather than listen to the orders he'd been listening to for so long.

Haven was a gorgeous man, and he was doing the right thing. That didn't mean Dimitri should allow himself to develop a crush on him. Besides, they probably wouldn't be together for long. No matter how much Haven wanted to protect Dimitri, Dimitri doubted it would be for the long run. Haven was a brave man, a man with honor, and it made sense that he wanted to be there for Dimitri, but eventually, he would realize they couldn't spend any more time together. They were too different for that, and Dimitri had to remember that.

He smiled and stretched, raising his arms high above his shoulders, enjoying the feeling of the sheets on his body. "I needed that," he commented.

"You needed what? A good night's sleep?" Haven asked.

When Dimitri looked at him, he was sitting on the edge of the mattress, his back to Dimitri. He was still wearing his clothes, as if he was afraid to be half-naked with Dimitri, or maybe it was because he'd been afraid someone would attack them during the night. Dimitri didn't know, and he wasn't about to ask. "A night in a bed. Don't get me wrong, I love the forest, and I love my wolves, but sleeping in a bed is way different, and way more comfortable." Even when he was in his shifted forms, he didn't sleep as well as he had the night before.

It didn't make sense that he had. The conclave was after him, and now, after Haven. Dimitri should have been too anxious to sleep, but somehow, Haven's presence next to him had helped. He'd slept like a baby, and he felt ready to face the world — and the conclave.

"I'm going to the bathroom," Haven said. "Stay in the bedroom. If you're hungry, I'll go grab something for you."

Dimitri rolled his eyes. "I wasn't about to run away or to go get food. I don't want humans to see me any more than you want that to happen." Sometimes, it made Dimitri sad, but he was so obviously not human that he couldn't spend time with humans who didn't know him. They would probably start screaming at the sight of his horns, and if that didn't do it, at his beard. He could cut it off, but it wouldn't be *him* anymore. It was part of him, just like the forest was, and he'd learned to live with it. Besides, the only people he didn't want to run away from him were the children, and they seemed to enjoy how different he looked most of the time.

They took turns in the bathroom, and even though Dimitri had showered the day before when they'd arrived at the motel, he showered again. There was no way for him to know when he would have access to hot water after today, and he was going to take advantage of it. He was going to make the most of it, because that was what his life was like. He always had to make the most of the situation he was in.

When he left the bathroom, Haven was waiting for him. He was ready, boots on his feet, his sword hanging at his side. Dimitri had wanted to ask how Haven had managed to get a room and whether the owner of the motel had thought Haven was human, but he didn't. He had no doubt Haven was used to doing things like that. He would have to, considering the work he did and the fact that he did it all over the world.

"Now what?" he asked

Haven shook his head. "I'm not sure." He'd appeared uncertain yesterday, and he still did.

Dimitri was surprised that emotion was still on his face. "We should probably separate," he said, even though he could think of nothing he wanted less. He didn't want to have to face the conclave or another hero. He wanted to feel protected the way he did with Haven, but it wasn't possible. Even if they stayed together for a while, they were too different.

Besides, from what Dimitri knew of Haven, Haven would eventually try to contact the conclave again to convince them to take him back. It might not work, but it also might, and then Dimitri would lose him. That was why he had to push away all the feelings he was starting to have for Haven and ignore them.

Haven shook his head. "You're not going anywhere without me."

"Things aren't going to be easy between us if you're this stubborn." Because Dimitri was stubborn, too.

Haven blinked. "Between us?"

Dimitri shrugged as he felt his cheeks heating. "You know what I mean. You want to stick with me, but I think it would be better if we went our separate ways. One of us will have to give up, and I don't know how we're going to decide who."

Haven crossed his arms over his chest, no doubt ready to fight it out, at least verbally, when the door banged open. A man barged in, his sword out, and Dimitri knew they'd run out of time.

The conclave had sent another hero, and he'd found them.

The hero looked around only for a second. Then Haven was on him, raising his sword, ready to defend Dimitri and himself. Dimitri sucked in a breath. The humans sleeping in the other rooms would realize something was happening from the noise, and if they came in, it would be a disaster. They had to leave, but Dimitri doubted the new hero would allow them to go anywhere.

He looked at the forest. He could run. He could leave Haven behind and hope the other hero wouldn't hurt him.

He couldn't abandon Haven, though, especially not in this situation. Haven might not be able to live with himself if he killed Dimitri, but the same went for Dimitri. He couldn't leave, not after what Haven had done for him.

"The forest," Haven snapped as he raised his sword again, meeting the one that was coming toward his face and blocking it in a clang of metal against metal.

Dimitri looked out the open door. So far, there was no one in the parking lot, but it wouldn't last for long. "What about you?"

"I'll be right behind you."

Dimitri could only trust Haven, so he threw himself out the door. He ran toward the forest, relieved they'd chosen a motel that was right next to it. He knew where they were, and they might just manage to escape if they were lucky—and fast.

His wolves were already there. He wasn't surprised they'd wanted to be close to him, even though he hadn't slept with them. They stepped forward as one as he stumbled into the forest, and he sucked in a breath, wondering if he should use them against the hero.

He didn't have the opportunity to do that because Haven and the hero barged into the forest right behind him. Haven was running, but as soon as they were out of sight from the motel, he turned and faced the hero again. They could try to outrun the man, but Dimitri doubted it would do them any good.

"What are you doing?" the hero asked.

"Protecting a man who doesn't deserve to die," Haven snapped, pushing forward until the hero's back was against the tree.

The hero ducked and twisted, moving in a circle around Haven until Haven's back was against the tree instead of his. "Stop that. He's a supernatural creature. He deserves to die."

Haven shook his head and attacked again.

Dimitri held his breath. He wanted to help, but this was a two-man fight. Besides, Dimitri wouldn't know what to do

with a sword. He never used weapons. He never killed anyone himself. Maybe it was a coward's way, but he'd found
that was what worked best for him and for the children, and
unfortunately, it hadn't prepared him for the present situation.

"We can kill him together," the hero said.

Haven shook his head. "He did nothing wrong. He doesn't
deserve to die. Let him go."

"You know I can't do that. If you don't want to kill him, let
me do it. We'll tell the conclave we did it together, and you'll
be allowed to come back."

There was a hint of desperation in the new hero's voice,
and it made Dimitri realize the man probably knew Haven.
They might even be friends, and Dimitri loathed the fact that
two friends were fighting over him, over whether or not they
should kill him. He didn't want Haven to lose anyone from
his past, even though it was inevitable.

Haven shook his head. "You will *not* kill him, and neither
will I." His voice was strong and steady, not one hint of hesitation in it.

Dimitri hadn't realized how much he expected Haven to
say yes and to kill him until now, and his knees almost buck-
led with relief, so much that he had to hold himself up against
the closest tree. Of course Haven didn't want him to die. That
was why Haven was in this situation to begin with.

"I don't want to kill you," the hero said.

"Then don't. Let us go."

The fact that both of them were barely panting as they
fought was surprising, and Dimitri knew he wouldn't be as
good at it as they were. He wasn't a warrior, even though he'd
managed to fight off a few heroes over the years. He was a
runner, and he could feel the need to do just that crawling
under his skin.

He sucked in a breath when Haven launched himself

forward, his sword extended. It sank into the other hero's thigh, and the hero cried out, stumbling back. Dimitri took a step toward him, maybe to help him, he wasn't sure, but Haven was already moving without giving the hero a second glance. He took Dimitri's hand and pulled him in the opposite direction. "We have to run."

So Dimitri ran.

Haven was panicking. He had no idea how to get out of this situation.

He'd never had to fight against another hero, not outside training, and it wasn't the same thing by a long shot. He hadn't wanted to wound Mather, but there was no going back now. He hoped it would slow his fellow hero for a moment, but it wouldn't give them enough time to run away, not when he couldn't make a portal. There just wasn't enough time. Haven wanted to hope Mather would allow them to leave and focus on his wound, but he knew better. He'd been wounded on a mission, too, yet he'd pushed through the pain and found his target. It was what they were trained to do, and Mather wasn't any different.

Haven and Dimitri ran through the forest. He let Dimitri guide him until they reached a spot that looked just like every other spot in the forest. It had to be different, though, because Dimitri had stopped. His wolves did, too, but they stayed away from them, something for which Haven was relieved. They might not have attacked him, but that didn't mean he was comfortable around them.

"What now?" he asked.

Dimitri was panting, and he raised a hand, telling Haven to give him a moment—a moment they didn't have. "We're going to hide."

He looked around. "Where? We're in the middle of the

forest."

Dimitri straightened and winked at him. "You're with a leshy. Do you really think I won't be able to hide us in the forest?"

Dimitri leaned down. He moved the foliage on the ground, and Haven's eyes widened when he saw there was something there. It took Dimitri another few seconds to clear it entirely. Then, he opened what looked like a tiny trapdoor.

The hole under it was dark, and Haven wasn't looking forward to spending any length of time there, but they didn't have a choice.

Dimitri nodded. "Go down. I'll be right behind you. I have to hide the door again."

This was it. Haven had to decide whether or not he trusted Dimitri. If he went down there, he would be vulnerable, and Dimitri would be able to kill him at any moment. If he stayed in the forest, Mather would probably kill him. Either way, Haven would be dead.

Unless Dimitri really was a good man who didn't want to hurt anyone.

Haven took that chance.

He wiggled his way into the hole, for once hating his wide shoulders and muscles. The passage had been made for Dimitri, who was as tall as Haven but also slimmer, and Haven almost didn't fit. Still, with a little effort, he managed to slide down to the bottom of the hole.

Then his eyes widened again.

He'd thought this was just a hole in the ground, but it was a lot more than that. Someone had dug a big hole, and it was filled with leaves and furs that made up a nice nest-like structure. There was no light, especially not after Dimitri closed the trapdoor. Haven could feel him move, and he allowed Dimitri to take his hand and pull him toward the nest. He had to move using touch, and it was uncomfortable, but he finally managed to settle down in the nest.

"Will he be able to find us?" he asked.

"I suppose anything is possible, but I doubt it. I told the wolves to stick around, just in case. You wounded him, so hopefully, he'll stay away from them."

Haven wasn't sure that would be the case. Mather knew as well as he did that leshy used wolves and bears, so he would find it curious that an entire pack of wolves was hanging around there. Hopefully, they would be discreet. Either way, he and Dimitri couldn't stay here long.

Haven sighed and leaned against the wall behind him. "What next?" he asked.

He felt Dimitri shrug. "I don't know. Do you really think he'll find us?"

"Eventually. We have to move." But Haven had never been on the run, and he had no idea where to start.

He did know how heroes went after people who were running, though. That was what he'd done for many years, so he probably could think backward and find a way to evade the conclave and any other hero they would send after them. He had to think, though. He had to forget that the conclave had been his home for so long. He needed to focus on what the conclave wanted him to do, on how wrong they were. They wanted to kill Dimitri, and now, Haven. They weren't family, not anymore, and maybe they never had been.

He cleared his throat. "Do you know anyone who can help?"

"Apart from the wolves?"

"Apart from them, yes. What about the people who take care of the children? Could they help us?"

There was no hesitation in Dimitri's voice when he answered. "No. I won't pull them into this. I never have, and I won't change that. They're human beings, and they're trying to do their best for the children. That's who they have to focus on, not me. I won't put them in danger."

"That's fine. I'm not asking you to." Although it was the only idea Haven had, so he wasn't sure what to do next.

Dimitri sighed, and to Haven's surprise, leaned against his shoulder. "I don't know what to do," Dimitri admitted. "But if your friend is going to find us, we have to leave."

"Eventually, yes." But Haven hoped that if they waited, Mather would go back. He would have to find someone to take care of his wound, and he couldn't spend hours in the forest ignoring it. If he didn't find Dimitri and Haven soon, he'd move on, at least for a while. That would be the only opening they'd have to leave their hiding place, and Haven intended to take advantage of that.

"We'll move soon," he declared.

"That's fine with me. You know him better than I do. You know what he'll do. Should we go now?"

"No. Give him time to look around and not find us. If he doesn't, he'll head out to get his wound looked at. That's when we need to go." Hopefully, it would be soon because Haven didn't like being stuck in this hole. He liked being hunted by the conclave even less, but there didn't seem to be a way out of it. He'd decided to protect Dimitri, and by doing so, the children Dimitri helped, and he wasn't going back on that decision.

He was doing the right thing—for once.

Dimitri was both relieved and terrified when they left the hole. He was relieved because being in that place so close to Haven without the possibility of putting some space between them had been difficult. Dimitri had thought he could prevent his crush on Haven from expanding, but now he realized how wrong he'd been.

He'd watched Haven fight against the other hero to save

him. Dimitri didn't know if what the hero had said was true, if he really would have told the conclave that he and Haven had killed Dimitri together, but if it was, then Haven had had a chance to get out of this. He could have killed Dimitri and gone back to the conclave and his old life without looking back. Instead, he'd wounded a man he possibly considered a friend, and he hadn't hesitated to do so. Dimitri didn't know what to think about that—Haven had been clear that he didn't think Dimitri should die, but this was different. Even though he didn't think Dimitri deserved to die, he didn't have to help him or to go against everything he knew to support him. Instead, he'd done exactly that, and it endeared him to Dimitri. Dimitri had liked him before, but he liked him even more now.

It wasn't only Haven's good looks, either. It was all of him, the way he listened to Dimitri, the way he was protecting him, the way he'd renounced everything he knew so Dimitri could have a chance, how he cared for the children even though he obviously didn't have any.

Dimitri didn't know what to think of Haven or what to do with him. He liked Haven, had a crush on him, wanted to be closer to him, but he also was confused. He knew nothing could come out of it, not when they were so different, but his body hadn't gotten that memo.

"Do you think we can leave now?" he asked, a hint of desperation in his voice.

"I think so. It's been several hours. I doubt Mather is still around." He got to his feet, almost hitting his head against the roof of the hole Dimitri had dug with the wolves. He swore, and Dimitri had to press his lips together so he wouldn't laugh.

"Stay here. I'll check if he's still around," Haven said, and his voice was authoritative, as if he knew Dimitri was going to protest.

Dimitri didn't. He stayed right where he was as Haven climbed up the hole and opened the trapdoor. They both knew that if the other hero was still around, he would easily get to Haven in this situation. Then he'd just had to wait for Dimitri to leave the hole. There was nowhere else Dimitri could go, nothing else he could do.

The hero wasn't there, though. Haven's entire body was tense, but he climbed out of the hole, closing the door behind himself. Dimitri waited, and it felt like an eternity to be alone in the dark. He was used to this—he'd lived here since he'd arrived in town to save the children—but the situation was different. He didn't know what was happening out there, except for the fact that someone was hunting him.

The trapdoor opened again, and Haven's head poked through. "You can come out. We should hurry before he comes back. There's no way to know when he left."

Dimitri scrambled out of the hole. One of the wolves came closer, butting her head against his thigh. He crouched and took the opportunity to pet her. He was going to miss them. He doubted he would see them again. By the time he came back to this area, they would no doubt be dead, their children having taken their place. It was the way it always went, and there was nothing Dimitri could do about it.

He buried his face in the wolf's fur, hugging her close. "Thank you," he murmured. "You did a lot for the children and me. I will be eternally grateful to you and the rest of the pack. I have to go now, though."

When he looked up, he found Haven looking down at him. Haven looked away, a trace of pink on his cheeks, but Dimitri didn't understand why he should be embarrassed. Haven wasn't the first person who was fascinated by the way Dimitri talked to the wolves. It was surprising he hadn't asked questions yet. He was apparently convinced that Dimitri controlled the wolves, and while Dimitri certainly could, he tried not to. The wolves might be animals, but they had a mind of their own, and they should be able to follow it without anyone ordering them around.

Dimitri got to his feet. "We can go," he said.

Haven nodded. "I think it would be for the best, yes. We should stick to our plan."

Dimitri blinked. "Our plan?"

Haven shuffled. "I know I said we shouldn't do this, but I think we should separate."

Dimitri's heart sank. "You said we should stick together."

"I changed my mind. Now, I want you to run away. I'll stay back to take care of Mather."

Dimitri wasn't even surprised that Haven was going to sacrifice himself to help him. He crossed his arms over his chest, and Haven tensed, probably sensing what Dimitri was about to say. "I'm not leaving you alone to face that guy."

"It's the best thing you can do. Don't you see? I know him. I know how he fights and his weaknesses. I'll take advantage of them, and hopefully, I'll manage to kill him while you run away. You need that extra time."

"What if he kills you?"

Haven shrugged. "Then I die. I've lived for a long time."

Dimitri was horrified. "You lived for a long time as a hero. That's not living. You deserve to have your life back, and that's not going to happen if you stay behind and fight that guy. I'm sorry, but no. I'm not leaving you behind."

Haven opened his mouth, no doubt to insist they did this, when the wolves around them tensed. Their heads snapped as one toward a spot in the woods, but before Dimitri and Haven could react, they were attacked again.

The hero was back.

This time, he made a beeline for Dimitri. Dimitri saw the sword swing, and he knew he wouldn't have the time to step out of its path. He closed his eyes, accepting death. Just like

Haven, he'd lived long enough, and he'd thought about this moment. He might be virtually immortal, but what he did for the children was dangerous, and he'd always expected something like this would happen eventually.

It looked like his time had come.

Pain flared in his leg. He opened his eyes to see that Haven had pushed the hero to the ground, and while the hero had managed to hurt Dimitri, it wasn't a mortal wound. Dimitri's thigh hurt like hell, and the injury mirrored the one Haven had inflicted on the hero, but Dimitri would live.

Whether or not he could run away was a different problem.

Dimitri didn't know what to do. He couldn't run away. There was no way he would make it, not with the pain pulsing in his thigh. There was only one way for him to escape this — he had to pray Haven would manage to win against the other hero, and he had to shift.

So he did just that. He shifted, thinking about a form that would be easy for Haven to grab with one hand and run away. He didn't shift often because it cost him a lot of energy, but right now, he had to do it.

It was strange. The world seen from this height felt alien, and Dimitri prayed the heroes wouldn't step on his small mouse form, so he moved closer to one of the trees, hoping Haven had seen him. He dragged his thigh behind, leaning against the trunk, and praying that this time, too, they would make it out of this alive. He didn't know what he would do if something happened to Haven.

Die, probably.

Chapter Six

Dimitri was gone, and Haven had no idea where he was. He hadn't managed to keep his focus on him when he became smaller, and now he didn't know what to do.

Well, in part, he *did* know. Mather was standing there, looking around. It was only a matter of time before he found Dimitri and tried to kill him again, and Haven couldn't allow that to happen.

He knew what he would have to do next. He would take care of Mather, one way or another, then he would find Dimitri and portal their asses out of here. The conclave could normally trace portals, but Haven had studied enough over the years to find a way to open one without them knowing. That way, they wouldn't know where he and Dimitri were going.

Because there was no way he was leaving Dimitri alone, not now that Dimitri was wounded. Haven had seen Mather hit him, then blue blood dripping from the wound. He'd been shocked for a second, never having killed a leshy and not expecting the color, but he'd managed to push Mather out of the way.

"Come on, Haven," Mather said, looking around. "You can't do this anymore. The conclave will kill you if you don't kill him."

"That doesn't mean I'll do it. What the conclave is doing is wrong."

"He's a supernatural creature. He kidnapped children and killed their parents."

"He took children to give them better families and killed

their abusers. That's what he did. The conclave knows that, too, but they don't want to admit it, because it would mean they were wrong."

That gave Mather pause, but not enough. "He probably lied to you. Come on. You know how they work. They would say anything to save their lives."

Haven would get nowhere with him. He had to kill him or wound him again, and talking things through wouldn't change anything. He might as well do it now.

He raised his sword, and Mather did, too, his expression shifting to stubbornness. "If you don't do it, I'll have to kill you, too," he warned.

"You can certainly try."

Haven attacked first. They'd fought against each other several times, always for training. They'd never held back, though, so Haven knew how Mather moved. That made it easier for him to understand what Mather's next move would be, but the same went for Mather. He knew the way Haven moved and thought, and he could easily anticipate Haven's next move.

Haven had to change the way he reacted. He wasn't sure how to do that, but he had to at least try.

Focusing on that, he feigned to the left, then struck to the right, aiming for Mather's heart. He didn't get to it, but he managed to cut into Mather's side, and blood appeared on his shirt.

Mather stumbled back. Not for long, though, and he raised his sword again.

The clang of metal against metal echoed in the forest. The wolves were still around, and from the corner of his eye, Haven saw one of them come closer to the tree where Dimitri had been earlier. Something tiny climbed onto the wolf's nose, and Haven's eyes widened when he saw it was a mouse. He'd known leshy could shift, but he hadn't realized they could become mice — there was no way this one was a normal animal, the way it was behaving.

The glint of Mather's sword made Haven snap his head back. He had to focus on Mather now that he knew where Dimitri was. Even if something happened to him and Mather managed to kill him, the wolves would take care of Dimitri. He was injured, but as long as he stayed away from Mather, he would manage to escape. He would heal, and he would run away.

Haven saw an opening only seconds later, and he took it. He forced the thought that he was killing a fellow hero away and struck, digging a deep hole in Mather's thigh — the one he hadn't wounded earlier.

Mather stumbled, and blood spurted out of the wound. They looked at each other, and Haven nodded. "I hit the femoral artery. You should get it checked out before you lose too much blood."

Mather's eyes were wide, but he knew it was the truth. They were all trained to recognize the wound.

He reached out, opening a portal, but Haven didn't stick around to look at what was going on. He turned toward the wolves, reaching for Dimitri. To his surprise, the wolf didn't growl at him or try to run away. Instead, it stayed still, and Haven managed to take Dimitri's small form. He raised it to his face so he could see Dimitri better, grimacing at the sight of the blue blood on Dimitri's fur. "How are you feeling?"

Dimitri shook his head. He couldn't answer, but they both knew they had to leave. Mather was gone, and his portal was closed, but they didn't have a lot of time.

Haven looked at the wolves. "You need to run away and hide. Others will come, and they won't be kind. I'll take care of him." He didn't know if the wolves understood him, but at least, he'd tried.

He raised his free hand, opening a portal. He felt the

energy drain out of him, but he couldn't think about that right now. Instead, he stepped through the portal, making sure it closed behind him before he relaxed. Once he did, he leaned down and set Dimitri on the ground.

Dimitri shifted right away, heavily leaning on his unhurt leg and grimacing. "Where are we?"

"Behind a motel I stayed at several years ago. I was here on a case." And he'd particularly liked the place. It was close to the forest and comfortable, and he'd been sorry when he'd had to leave.

"Will the conclave find us?"

"I doubt it. I couldn't stay in the motel they pointed me to. It was closed. I never told them that, though." The new motel had been more expensive than the conclave would have paid for, but he'd wanted the luxury for a few days. It came in handy now, even though he knew they wouldn't be able to stay here for long. At least they would be able to rest and check Dimitri's wound.

Haven wasn't sure what to do with Dimitri and his sword, though. He looked around, thinking he had to hide them in the forest. It didn't take him long to help Dimitri settle against a tree, and he left with the promise that Dimitri wouldn't try to run away. Even if he'd wanted to, Haven doubted he could. He was still bleeding, and that thought made Haven move faster.

He got a room, then went back to get Dimitri and his sword.

They were where he'd left them, and they headed to the room Haven was grateful they could access it from the outside. That way, if they were attacked again, it would be easier for them to leave.

Dimitri sat down as soon as they were in the room. His face was a mask of pain, and Haven knew they should hurry. He was losing quite a bit of blood, even though his femoral artery hadn't been hit.

"I'm going to have to cut your pants," he warned.

Dimitri looked down at his legs. "Not a problem. They're already cut up and dirty anyway. I doubt I can get this much blood out of them even if I wanted to fix them."

It was strange to think of the blue substance as blood, even though it had the same consistency.

Haven had to focus on what he was doing rather than on Dimitri's long legs. Dimitri's skin was pale, and it was covered with blue streaks. Haven cleaned the wound as well as he could and bandaged it with towels he found in the bathroom, but it wouldn't be enough.

He couldn't do this on his own. He'd never been on the run and hunted. He didn't know what it was like to be in this situation, and he wasn't prepared. He'd never thought something like this would happen to him, and he had no idea what was next. He had to protect Dimitri and make sure his wound healed the way it should, but how?

He needed help. He needed *Thor*.

CHAPTER SEVEN

Haven still wasn't sure why Thor had given him his phone number, but he had, which meant he probably expected Haven to call him eventually. That meant he would answer, which was what Haven hoped for. He was out of his depth, and he had to find a way out, both for him and Dimitri.

He allowed Dimitri to doze on one of the beds in the room and moved toward one of the windows. He peered outside, wishing he could step out to make this call. He didn't want to leave Dimitri alone, though, and just in case, he didn't want to be seen. That was why he'd drawn all the curtains. That way, even if the conclave managed to find them, they wouldn't know in which room they were.

Then he made the call.

It took a moment for Thor to answer, to the point that Haven wasn't sure he would. Then a voice Haven recognized came on the other side of the line. "Haven," Thor said.

Haven sucked in a breath. "Thor. I need help."

There was a pause, then Thor said. "Well, it's one of the reasons I gave you my number. What happened?"

"Why did you do it?" Haven asked instead of answering. He had to be sure Thor would help them and not give him and Dimitri back to the conclave, or worse, kill them himself. Haven didn't think that would happen, because Thor had more honor than the conclave. But just in case, he had to be sure. He couldn't be rash.

"What do you mean?" Thor asked.

"Why did you give me your number?" He'd gotten a text

from an unknown number a few days after Haven had let Thor and the others go. Haven had been confused, but he'd known it was a sign of trust, even though he doubted anyone would be able to find Thor and his friends through it. He'd cherished the number, even though he hadn't thought he would need it.

He'd been wrong.

"I'm indebted to you," Thor finally said.

"You're not."

"You let me and Cecil go. You could have killed us, or at least, fought us. We would have fought back, and we would have won, but we would have been in bad shape at the end of it. Instead, you realized the right thing to do was to let us go, and you did. *That's* why I'm in debt to you. I was able to focus on Cecil and help him instead of having to think about fighting you."

Haven didn't like the thought of anyone feeling indebted to him, but he wasn't about to argue any more than he already had. Hopefully, the way Thor felt about their situation would help.

He swallowed. "I need to make someone disappear."

"Disappear as in you want me to kill them?"

That startled Haven, even though it shouldn't have. Thor was a professional killer, after all. "No. I don't want you to kill him. I want you to help him. The conclave is after him, and we've already run from one of the heroes twice. He's wounded, and we can't run anymore."

"Why don't you tell me this story from the beginning?"

"There's not much to say. I was sent to kill a leshy. The conclave told me he was killing parents and taking their children away. Instead, I found out that he was killing the children's abusers and finding them a new home. I contacted the conclave to tell them what was going on, and they told me to kill him anyway."

"And you refused."

"I didn't kill him, no. They sent another hero, and while I managed to wound him, he also wounded Dimitri. He needs a safe place."

"What about you?"

"I'll go back." Because against all the odds, Haven still wondered if he could convince the conclave, or at least a few members, that this was the right thing to do. The conclave had to change the way they viewed supernatural creatures, and that wouldn't happen if no one pushed. Right now, Haven was apparently the only hero who believed that not all supernatural creatures need to be killed on sight. If he didn't try, no one would.

"I think you should go with him," Thor said.

"I'll go with him to wherever he has to go, but then I'll leave."

"Whatever you say." But Thor didn't sound convinced.

Thor didn't know Haven, and Haven didn't insist. Nothing would make Thor believe him anyway.

"I'm going to send you an email with the directions to one of Tryg's caves. You can hide in there until we come up with a plan."

"Are you sure?" Because Tryg hadn't seemed to like Haven very much. Of course, neither had Thor, yet here he was, helping him.

"I'm sure. I know where you are because I traced your phone, which by the way, you should leave behind as soon as you memorize the email, and one of the caves isn't far from your position. No one will find you there, and even if they do, they won't be able to come in. The cave is equipped with an alarm system. You and your friend will be safe."

"Thank you." Haven still wasn't sure that getting Thor involved was the right thing to do, but he knew it was the only thing he could do. He had no other way to save Dimitri, and right now, that was the most important thing for him. He should have let Dimitri go as soon as he'd found him. Instead, he'd stuck around to make sure Dimitri wasn't lying to him, and that had given the conclave time to realize what was happening and send someone else. If it weren't for Haven, Dimitri would be far away from here, safe. Instead, he was snuggled in one of the beds behind Haven, no doubt in pain, and it was Haven's fault. That meant Haven had to find a way to save him, and hopefully, he just had.

Once again, Dimitri had no idea what was happening. The only thing he knew was that Haven was with him and had taken care of him, and right now, that was the only thing he cared about.

Haven wouldn't allow anyone to hurt him. He'd showed it time and time again, even though they'd met only yesterday, and Dimitri trusted him to take care of him, especially now that he was wounded. He realized it was probably selfish — Haven wanted to go back to the conclave from what Dimitri had heard during his conversation on the phone — but Dimitri couldn't bring himself to care. He didn't want to be alone. He didn't want to have to take care of himself. He was used to doing just that, and he hadn't had someone to take care of him in too long. Now that he did, he didn't want it to end.

His thigh hurt. Haven had wrapped it up as best as he could, but he'd muttered they needed more. Dimitri had never been good with pain and blood, and now he was frightened.

"We're moving," Haven said.

Dimitri blinked at him, realizing he wasn't on the phone anymore. "What do you mean?"

"That we're moving," Haven repeated. "I just talked to someone I trust. They have a hiding place close by. We can stay there until they reach us."

"I think I need a healer." Unfortunately, they weren't common. Dimitri knew several of them, but he didn't think any were in the area, which was a problem.

"Thor said there was a first aid kit in the cave. You don't have to worry about that. As soon as we're there, I'll clean it up and stitch it, and I'll give you pills to fend off any infection."

Dimitri tried to sit up and grimaced at the pain that shot down his leg. "Cave?"

"I'll explain as soon as we're there, okay?"

Dimitri nodded. "Will you open a portal?"

Haven hesitated.

That gave Dimitri the answer he wanted, but he still waited for Haven to say it out loud.

"I can probably open a portal once we're close by, but not from here. Opening the portal before took a lot of energy out of me, and I don't want to be too weak, just in case."

Dimitri frowned. "I thought heroes used portals all the time? How can you if they weaken you?"

"We do use portals all the time, but this wasn't a normal portal. The conclave can follow us using the portals we open, at least the normal ones. That way, they know where we are and where we want to go. I had to make sure they wouldn't find us through this one, though, and getting rid of the spell they use to trace us wasn't easy."

Dimitri had never known about that, but it made sense. The heroes were the conclave's military wing. They had to keep them under control if they didn't want things to get out of hand, and that was what might happen if Haven could contact other heroes and explain what was happening. They'd realize that what the conclave was doing was wrong. They might rebel, and that was the last thing the conclave wanted.

Dimitri nodded. "I'm sorry you had to use your energy that

way."

"I'm not. I would do it again if it meant keeping you safe. But as long as we're not under attack, we should try to get closer to the cave before I open a portal. It would be even better if you could walk all the way there, though." Haven's gaze moved to the wound on Dimitri's leg.

Dimitri forced himself to get up from the bed. It hurt. There was no denying that, but Dimitri did everything he could to keep his expression under control. He didn't want Haven to realize how much pain he was in. If he did, Haven would insist on opening a portal, and after what he'd just said, Dimitri wasn't going to allow him to do that. Haven needed all his energy in case they were attacked again, and Dimitri could walk a few miles.

Hopefully, the cave wouldn't be that far, though.

"What about this room?" Dimitri asked, looking around. He'd been looking forward to another warm shower, and he doubted he would get that in a cave.

"We can just leave it. I used a false identity anyway. Don't worry about it. Only worry about getting to the cave."

So that was what Dimitri did. As soon as he was on his feet, he had to focus on not stumbling and not showing the pain he felt every time he took a step. It made his wound pulse to the rhythm of his heart, and he wondered if he might lose the leg. It sure felt like it was about to fall off, even though he knew that wasn't the case.

Haven had probably been through worse, yet Dimitri doubted he'd complained. He was a hero, and he was strong. Dimitri had to be just as strong. He'd dragged Haven into this, and now they could only rely on each other, at least until Haven's friends arrived. Haven wanted to protect Dimitri, although Dimitri still didn't understand why, and Dimitri had to protect Haven.

Well, he had to do everything he could to make Haven's

life easier, at the very least. He doubted he would be any good in a fight, especially now, but he could allow Haven to focus on their surroundings instead of on himself and his leg.

He gritted his teeth and walked for what felt like hours. He didn't know how long it had been, though, but when he stumbled, Haven was there, holding him up every single time and making sure he was okay before they walked on.

Until he didn't let Dimitri go.

Dimitri almost fell on his face, and Haven caught him once again. Dimitri's back hit Haven's chest, and before he could say anything about it, Haven reached down and hooked an arm under Dimitri's knees. He hauled him up, and Dimitri's first instinct was to wrap his arms around Haven's neck. Haven held him close, and Dimitri saw the way he gritted his teeth when he opened another portal.

"I could have walked," he said.

Haven shook his head. "I should have realized how much pain you were in. I'm not going to let you walk, not when it's obvious your leg is hurting. Besides, we're closer to the cave now. It'll be fine."

Dimitri hoped it would be. He kept an eye on their surroundings as Haven stepped through the portal. The place where they stepped out of it looked very much the same as the place they'd just left, but obviously, it wasn't. They were still in the middle of the forest, though, and Dimitri briefly closed his eyes, inhaling the familiar smells. As long as he was in a forest, he was home, no matter where he was.

Haven was careful with Dimitri, keeping his gait steady so as not to jostle his leg. Dimitri still didn't know what to think of it, but before he could start obsessing over it, Haven walked into a cave.

Dimitri held his breath. Was this the place where they were going to have to wait? Because to him, it looked like a normal cave. He'd spent countless nights sleeping in caves just like this one, and while he was used to it, he'd hoped there would be more to it, like maybe a nice couch or something. He would make do, though.

To his surprise, Haven walked toward the back of the cave. It looked just like the rest of the cave to Dimitri, but Haven obviously knew something Dimitri didn't.

Sure enough, he found a pad on the wall. Haven punched in a code, and Dimitri's eyes widened when part of the cave in front of them moved. Haven didn't hesitate to step in, and Dimitri held his breath as he tried to take everything in.

They were still in a cave, all right, but this one was as different as the one they just been in as day and night. The walls were still stone, but it looked more like a cozy apartment, one of those Dimitri had seen on some of the magazines he'd found that campers left behind in the forest.

It was a cave, but it had a couch, and hopefully, it also had hot water.

Haven was worried about the wound on Dimitri's thigh, so he headed to the bathroom. It took him a few tries to find it, but eventually, he did, and he was relieved to see it was state-of-the-art. Dimitri would be able to take a bath and keep his thigh out of the water. He would be happy. It was better than the shower at the motel where they'd stayed the day before.

He gently put Dimitri down on the closed toilet, then looked under the sink for the first aid kit Thor had mentioned. Dimitri was in pain, his expression tight, his face even paler than it had been before. Even his beard seemed to slump, and Haven found himself wanting to find a way to make everything better.

Luckily, there were painkillers in the first aid kit.

He gave Dimitri a few with a glass of water he filled at the sink, then went to work to unwrap the wound. It would hurt, and he had to distract Dimitri. "How did you start?"

"How did I start what?" Dimitri answered, his body tense under Haven's hands.

"Saving children. I mean, there are a lot of people in the world, and I doubt many of them do what you do. Why did you decide to do it?"

Dimitri sucked in a breath, and Haven expected him not to answer. Instead, he said. "I was an abused child myself. I'm not a full-blooded leshy. My father was human, and my mother thought he loved her. And maybe he did, at least until she had his child. I never talked to him about this, of course, but I suspect he loved the strange part of my Mother. She was obviously not human, and my father loved that. But then she had me, and everything was different. I look like her. I couldn't pass for a human, either, and I think my father resented me for that. So he decided he didn't want my mother anymore. It was too much hassle, and I guess he hoped she would just disappear. And she did, for a while, until she went back to him and left me there when she left again."

"She left you with him?"

Dimitri snorted. "She did. I don't know why, or what happened to her."

Haven almost looked up, but instead, he focused on the wound. Now wasn't the time to be outraged at what Dimitri had gone through. "She never came back for you?"

"She didn't. That left my father with a child that didn't look human but looked enough like him that he couldn't deny I was his son. He hated me, and he made sure I knew it. He kept me locked in the basement so no one would ever see me, and he took his anger out on me. As soon as I was old enough, I ran. I've never seen him again, and I'm glad he's dead. But when I saw another child being abused, I intervened, even though I didn't know what I was doing. I couldn't let the child get hurt. That's how it started. I wasn't planning on doing what I do now. It was an instinct in the beginning, but I'm happy I did it. There are so many children in need in the world. I'm over what happened to me when I was a child, but I think this is the best way to keep that memory alive. I can never forget what my father did to me, and I use that to save other children."

Haven wasn't surprised. Dimitri was the kind of man who would go through something as horrible as being abused and come out of it stronger. Of course he wanted to save children. He was an honorable man, someone who didn't care about his well-being as much as he cared about the children.

Haven had to remind himself that Dimitri was a supernatural creature while he was a hero. They were natural enemies, and while that was mostly because of the conclave, Haven couldn't allow himself to forget it. They didn't fit together. The fact that they were even spending time together was only because of what was happening, not because they wanted it. No matter how much Haven liked Dimitri, how much respect he had for him, he had to keep his feelings in a place where they wouldn't grow.

He finished cleaning the wound while Dimitri talked about his past. He didn't ask many questions, happy to let Dimitri chatter. The wound was clean, and the stitches would hold. It would take a while for it to heal, but now that he knew Thor was coming, Haven was more positive about Dimitri's chances of making it. Once he was healed, he would go out there and save more children. It was his life's calling, and he was clearly more than happy to do it.

Haven got to his feet and washed his hands. "I'm going to let you take a bath. Just make sure you don't get the wound wet. I'll be in the kitchen putting something together for when you're done."

He moved to leave, but Dimitri caught his wrist. "Thank you," he murmured.

"You have nothing to thank me for."

"But I do. If it hadn't been for you, I would be dead right now. So yes, I'm going to thank you. I know you went against everything you've ever been taught to help me, and I'm grateful for it." He squeezed Haven's wrist, then let go, leaving a trail of warmth behind.

Haven shook his head. He couldn't think about everything he'd lost. He still hoped that eventually the conclave would realize what was going on and that they would change their minds. They had to. Haven couldn't lose everything he'd been working toward for hundreds of years. He couldn't think that the conclave had become so bad that they thought every single supernatural creature had to die, whether they deserved it or not.

He knew the truth, though, and while he would manage to push it down at the back of his mind at least for now, he knew it wouldn't last long. Eventually, he would have to face what the conclave had become, and what was next for him.

First, though, food.

CHAPTER EIGHT

Dimitri always felt better after a hot shower, but this was even better. His thigh hurt, but the painkillers were doing their job, and he'd managed to take a bath, something that hadn't happened in decades. All in all, he knew the situation could be worse, so he wasn't going to complain.

He stretched, looking down at his clothes on the floor. He had to put them back on even though they were dirty, bloody, and torn. He didn't have a change of clothes, not since he and Haven hadn't stopped to pick it up. It was still in the forest, and he suspected it would stay there. He wasn't about to put the pants back on, though, and he also wasn't looking forward to wearing dirty underwear, so he poked around in the bathroom, opening drawers and hoping to find something.

Luckily, he did.

He wasn't sure who the cave belonged to, but whoever they were, it was well prepared. Dimitri found several packs of new underwear in one of the drawers, as well as socks. There were also new clothes, in two different sizes. One size was a bit too short for his legs, but it fit, while the other was way too large. He had to choose, and he went with the smaller short clothes. He could always change if he couldn't move well in them.

Once he was dressed, he felt better—and hungry. He left the bathroom, looking around, still wondering who had built the place. Who needed a place like this to hide? And how hadn't Dimitri ever known about caves like these? He lived in the forest, and he could have done with such a place.

He shook his head. He didn't have the money to build anything like this. His *job* didn't pay at all, and he was lucky his wolves and bears didn't mind feeding him when he was working. The underground groups he worked with also helped him when it came to money, even though he didn't like depending on them. All in all, though, he made it work. He had a few places in the forest in which he stayed when he was there, and they were nice. He was doing well.

Nowhere as well the owner of this place, though.

Dimitri didn't have to go far to find Haven. Apart from the bathroom and another room or two, the cave was one big room. There was a bed in the middle of it, while the kitchen was to the side. Haven was there, cooking. Dimitri hadn't expected to walk in on that. When Haven had said he was going to put something together, Dimitri had expected a sandwich or something like that. Instead, Haven was cooking, and it smelled delicious.

Dimitri's stomach growled so loud that Haven heard it and turned to look at him. He gestured at the island, under which were two stools. "Why don't you sit down? It's almost ready. I forgot to ask if you're allergic to anything or if there was something you don't eat."

"I'm fine with whatever. I usually eat a lot of meat and roots, since I live in the forest, but I'm ready to try whatever it is you're cooking. When I have the money and the opportunity, I eat in human restaurants and diners." He pulled on his beard. "Of course, that's not easy, either, considering how I look. I make it work, though."

By that, he meant that he usually went as an animal. It was easier to sneak in and out as a mouse, but he always left money behind because he didn't want to steal. It was kind of strange for him to care about that when he didn't care about killing people, but it was the way it was.

"It's nothing elaborate," Haven said, rubbing the back of

his neck. "Just some spaghetti. We're lucky Tryg keeps food in here. I guess we should thank him for that when we see him."

Dimitri was curious about whoever this Tryg was. "He's another hero?"

Haven snorted. "God, no. He's a professional assassin."

Dimitri blinked at him. "A professional assassin? And you're friends with him?"

Haven turned back to the stove. "I'm not friends with him and Thor. I was supposed to kill Thor a few months ago. The conclave sent me when we got a call that someone had caught him. He's a professional assassin, too, or rather, he was. He retired from that kind of job, but he's Tryg's handler."

"You say you were supposed to kill him. Do you make it a habit of not killing the people the conclave sends you to kill?"

Haven slightly turned so he could look at Dimitri and grimaced. "Not usually, no. I never thought about the conclave's orders much until I met Thor. Then I realized that the person who had called me was trying to use me and the conclave to get rid of him. Eventually, the guy was killed, and Thor came out victorious. I wasn't about to call the conclave on him, not when I realized what had happened. I let him and his boyfriend and friends go."

Dimitri leaned back in his chair and stared at Haven. He didn't understand him. He was a hero. He worked for the conclave, and like most heroes, he'd worked for them a long time, probably hundreds of years. He should be brainwashed. Dimitri had thought he was an exception, that maybe Haven hadn't killed him because he hadn't been able to deny that what Dimitri was doing was a good thing. Apparently, though, it wasn't the first time something like this happened, and that made Dimitri wonder.

Haven might not make it a habit to save people he was supposed to kill, but he sure made it sound like it. He had a conscience, something Dimitri hadn't thought heroes had. He didn't know exactly how becoming a hero worked — no one beyond heroes and their conclave did — but he'd always thought that the process took away something of the human side of the heroes. He hadn't believed older heroes had been horrible human beings before becoming heroes. Apparently, he'd been wrong. Either that, or something had gone wrong in the process during which Haven had become a hero.

But Haven couldn't help what he was, just like Dimitri couldn't. Everyone knew that heroes were born that way. They were human until they agreed to become heroes, and once they were heroes, they couldn't go back. It was for life, and they were immortal, like many of the creatures they hunted. What had happened, then? How had Haven found his conscience? Was it only because of what had happened with Thor? Or was there more to it?

Dimitri couldn't help but wonder if Haven was leaving the conclave or if he still had hope that things would work out. Dimitri doubted it, and he didn't think Haven truly believed it, either, but it was harder for him to wrap his mind around that. Dimitri had always known the conclave was evil. Haven, on the other hand, had believed in them until recently. The conclave and the other heroes had been his entire life, and it had to be hard to leave them behind, especially in this kind of situation.

Besides, Dimitri might be wrong. The conclave might be different now.

He cleared his throat. "What now?" He felt like he'd been asking that question again and again lately, but he had to ask it. He had to know what was next, both for him and Haven. They couldn't allow the conclave to catch up to them, but the conclave was always hard to leave behind, maybe especially so now that Dimitri was traveling with a hero.

Things were awkward when they sat down to eat, although maybe that was all on Haven. He wasn't used to this. Even when he ate with the heroes, the chatter always was about missions and the way they were ridding the world of evil. He couldn't exactly talk to Dimitri about that, though, and if he was honest with himself, he didn't know what he *could* talk about with Dimitri. They weren't on vacation. They weren't having a good time. They were on the run from the people Haven had considered his family for hundreds of years, and Haven didn't know how to behave. He doubted that anything he could say would make the situation better, but he also didn't want Dimitri to feel guilty. It wasn't his fault that Haven was on the run. Haven was running because he'd refused to do the wrong thing, and he would do it again if he had to. He was ready to protect Dimitri until he was sure Dimitri was safe, even if it meant leaving everything behind.

But he was going to fight to keep his life.

He was convinced the conclave wasn't as bad as Dimitri thought it was. There had to be someone good sitting on the conclave, someone who would understand. Haven couldn't allow the other ones to take over — the ones who couldn't see further than their belief that all supernatural creatures were bad. He had to find the good side of the conclave, and he had to appeal to them. He had to make sure they understood that Dimitri was doing the right thing, even though he might be doing it the wrong way. But if it weren't for Dimitri, no one would be helping the children, and that was why the conclave and the heroes had been created in the first place. They were here to help humanity. It was their mission, the reason they were born. Instead, Dimitri was doing their job for them, and it wasn't a good thing.

"You didn't answer my question," Dimitri pointed out.

Haven didn't look at him. "That's because I don't know

how to answer. I don't know what's next except that we have to wait for Thor to arrive. He'll help you. He has an extensive number of friends and people who can help him make you disappear. You'll be safe with him."

"Even though he's a professional assassin?"

"He's retired, but yes, even though." Because Haven had looked into it when he'd gone back to the conclave, and he'd found out that Thor and the people he worked with only killed people who deserved it. They went after rapists, killers, human traffickers, drug dealers. They went after people who didn't deserve to live, which was why even though Haven wasn't sure he understood why they were doing it, he couldn't berate them for it. It was also why he was convinced Dimitri would be safe with them.

For whatever reason, though, he found himself reluctant over the thought of leaving Dimitri behind.

He knew it had to do with the stupid crush he was developing on the leshy. He couldn't allow himself to give in, though. He had to focus on the situation, on what would happen if the conclave caught them, especially Dimitri. Haven might be ready to die, but Dimitri didn't deserve to. Haven would make sure he didn't, even if it was the last thing he did.

He hoped it wouldn't be.

"What about you? What will you do when your friend arrives?" Dimitri asked, his voice a whisper.

"I don't know. I'll make sure you're safe, and I'll help you escape from the conclave. You'll have to lay low for a bit, but you should be fine. I'm sure they'll try to find you again in a few years, but you're used to it. They caught you by surprise this time. I know you won't make the same mistake twice."

Dimitri shook his head. "The conclave didn't catch me by surprise. *You* did. I still know how you found me, but I'm grateful it was you. I'm not sure I would have been able to escape if I'd had to face a different hero. They would have killed me on sight, not caring about the girl I was carrying. You didn't. You listened to me. You're the only one who did that." Dimitri reached for Haven's hand on the table, but he stopped inches from taking it.

Haven stared at their hands, so close yet so far. He wanted Dimitri to take his hand, but he couldn't ask for it.

"I want to know what you'll do," Dimitri continued. He moved his hand away and took his fork again.

Haven shrugged. "I'll go back to the conclave. It's where I belong, and I'm still not sure that I can't change it. I want to at least try."

"You disobeyed orders, and from what you told me, it happened twice. You saved a supernatural creature. The conclave won't be happy. You know what they do when they're not happy."

Haven knew *exactly* what they did, and he didn't like that Dimitri did, too. Dimitri had a deep knowledge of the conclave, something a supernatural creature shouldn't have. Haven supposed it made sense, though. From the information he'd found in the file he'd been given on Dimitri, the conclave had been after him for centuries. They'd tangled several times, and while Dimitri had managed to escape every time, he'd obviously gathered information on the conclave as he did so. He knew who they were, how they behaved.

He knew they were wrong.

"The conclave is the only thing I've known since I became a hero," Haven quietly explained. "I know they won't be happy. Hell, this was my last chance. They wanted to make sure I could do the job after I let Thor go. I'll be fine, though. Eventually I'll be able to make the conclave see they were wrong, and they'll allow me to stay on."

Dimitri looked at him like he didn't quite believe him, and Haven couldn't help but share that feeling. No matter what he was saying, no matter how much he wanted it to happen, he didn't actually have much hope that the conclave would listen to him. Even if there were one or two conclave members who might be on his side, the majority of them wouldn't. They'd demand his head on a pike, and knowing them — they would get it.

CHAPTER NINE

When Dimitri woke up the next day, his thigh was on fire, or at least, that was what it felt like. He knew that wasn't the case. He'd made sure to take both painkillers and antibiotics the day before so that it couldn't be infected. That didn't stop it from hurting, though, and he grimaced before he even moved from the bed.

Then he realized that what had woken him was Haven cooking breakfast. He was also *humming*.

Haven didn't seem to have realized Dimitri was awake, and Dimitri took a moment to observe him. He had his back to Dimitri as he worked on the stove, and from the smell, it was bacon.

Dimitri hadn't eaten bacon in ages, and his stomach growled. It didn't growl as loud as it had the day before, though, and Haven didn't hear it. That meant he didn't turn around, and Dimitri took a moment to assess how he was feeling.

He was in pain. His legs hurt, both the one he'd injured and the other one, possibly because he wasn't used to running around in the forest the way he had. The worst part was his injury. His thigh pulsed, and he felt like if he moved, it might just fall off. He knew that was ridiculous, so he gritted his teeth and swung his legs to the side of the bed to get up.

"What are you doing?"

Of course, this was the moment Haven had chosen to notice that Dimitri was awake. He put down the wooden spatula he'd been using and rushed to Dimitri's side, and even though Dimitri wanted to brush him off, he didn't.

He knew they didn't have a lot of time together. That was probably for the best, considering he still wasn't sure he could trust Haven, but he was going to regret not having Haven in his life. To his own surprise, he realized he would *miss* Haven.

He wasn't sure why. Dimitri admired him because he'd had the courage to go against everything he'd been taught. He was changing, becoming a better man because he knew it was the right thing to do. Or maybe he'd been a good man all along and it had been buried deep under the hero bullshit. Dimitri didn't know, and he wasn't sure he would ever find out. If Haven went back to the conclave, Dimitri knew what would happen to him. He suspected Haven did, too, yet he was going to try. Dimitri didn't know whether it was foolish or brave, and at this point, he didn't think it mattered. Whatever the reason behind it, Haven *was* going back to the conclave, and Dimitri wouldn't see him again after that.

Haven knelt in front of Dimitri and reached for his leg. "You're in pain, aren't you?"

Dimitri forced a smile on his face. "I've been better, that's for sure."

"I'll give you some painkillers, but I want you to eat something first. They can really hurt your stomach."

He was worried, but not just because Dimitri was wounded and, therefore, would slow him down. No, he was also worried that Dimitri was in pain and would feel sick.

Dimitri couldn't help it—he reached out for Haven, stroking Haven's cheekbone with his fingertips. Haven froze and looked at Dimitri with wide eyes, and Dimitri wondered what was happening. He had no idea what he was doing, and he doubted Haven knew, either.

Holding his breath, Dimitri leaned closer. He'd wanted to kiss Haven since they'd met, but he hadn't thought it possible. He'd thought they were enemies, but he didn't believe that anymore. Haven *wasn't* his enemy. He didn't know what Haven was, but maybe if they kissed, he would find out.

He gave Haven plenty of time to move away, but instead, Haven's gaze lowered to Dimitri's lips, and he licked his own. He wanted this as much as Dimitri, didn't he?

Dimitri leaned even closer.

Then the oven dinged.

Haven jerked away. He got to his feet, not looking at Dimitri. "Come on. You should eat breakfast before I give you the painkillers. I don't want your stomach to be upset."

Right now, it wasn't Dimitri's stomach that was upset. He wanted to kiss Haven, and he was pretty sure Haven wanted to kiss him, too. It didn't make sense because of who and what they were, but then nothing in this situation made sense. Dimitri should have already been on the run or dead. Instead, he was with Haven, and he had no idea how to situation would end. He didn't even know how the *day* would end. Certainly not with a kiss, from what he'd seen, though.

He reached out, offering Haven his hand. Haven hesitated, but in the end, he took Dimitri's hand and pulled him to his feet, steadying him when Dimitri stumbled. They stayed still for a moment, and then, Haven stepped away. "You should use the bathroom. I'll start plating the food."

Dimitri watched him walk away. He wanted to call him back, to tell him that he didn't care that they were different, but he didn't. He wasn't sure he could trust Haven, but even if he did, he wasn't the one who had the most to lose if something happened between them. Yes, he might lose part of his heart when Haven decided to go back, but Haven stood to lose his life as he knew it. He stood to lose everything—his family, what he'd worked for and had known for hundreds of years.

Dimitri suspected he'd already lost that and that he didn't want to admit it, but that was something Haven would have to work out for himself.

Instead of saying anything, Dimitri went to the bathroom. He washed his face, used the toilet, washed his hands, then stood and examined himself in the mirror.

His hair was tangled and in need of a brush, and his beard should be trimmed, but it was nothing urgent. He could stay like this for a few more hours, the time to eat and allow the painkillers to take effect. Then he would attempt to look more human — or as human as he could.

"When is your friend coming?" he asked as he joined Haven at the table.

Haven shrugged one shoulder. "I don't know. I don't even know where they are. He said to hunker down and wait for them, and that's what we're going to do." Haven narrowed his eyes and glared at Dimitri. "You weren't thinking of running away, were you?"

Dimitri snorted. "It's kind of hard to run away when you can't walk well. So, no. I wasn't planning on running away. I was just curious. I still can't wrap my mind around the fact that someone you were supposed to kill is now helping you."

Haven looked away, his cheeks slightly pink. "I'm not sure why he's doing it, either. He says he's in debt since I allowed him and his boyfriend to leave. I don't know. Maybe he truly is in debt to me, although I don't like to think of the situation that way. I don't want anyone to be in debt to me."

"Yet it came in handy in this situation." And Dimitri felt that he was in debt to Haven, too. After all, Haven had saved his life, and he was still doing it. He was taking care of him, making sure he had food and that his thigh healed correctly. Sure, Dimitri could have done all of that on his own in the forest, but it was much more comfortable in the cave, and he felt safer.

Yes, he was indebted to Haven, but after what Haven had just said, he knew better than to point that out. It would push

Haven away, and Dimitri didn't want that, even though he wasn't planning on taking the next step. If Haven wanted to be with him, wanted anything to happen, he would have to make that decision himself.

Haven didn't like feeling confused, and that was exactly how he was feeling right now. He wasn't sure what had happened between him and Dimitri earlier when he'd rushed to Dimitri's side when Dimitri tried to get up.

It had been too long since Haven had been intimate with anyone, and he wasn't thinking about sex. Intimacy wasn't sex, and for whatever reason, he was sharing that with Dimitri. It had to do with the fact that they were on the run, with everything they'd been through together already. Whatever the reason, Haven had to make sure nothing happened. It would be too easy to give in. He had to remind himself that Dimitri was hurt, and even more important, that Dimitri was a supernatural creature while Haven was a hero. Even if Haven managed to convince the conclave they should give Dimitri a chance, there couldn't be anything between the two of them. Haven would go back to work, while Dimitri had things to do for the children. But if Haven *didn't* manage to convince the conclave, he would probably die, and he didn't want to make the situation even harder on Dimitri.

No, this was a bad idea all around, and Haven had to keep that in mind.

Dimitri got to his feet and stumbled, and Haven acted on impulse, not thinking about it. He shot to his feet and took Dimitri's arm, guiding him back to the chair. "What do you think you're doing?"

Dimitri glared at him. "What does it look like I'm doing? I want to help. You cooked, so it's only fair that I clean up."

"You're wounded. You need to stay off your feet. I'll take

care of the cooking and cleaning." Because Haven loved it.

He might not have been intimate with anyone in a long time, but it had been even longer since he'd had anything resembling a normal routine. The last time had been when he lived with his parents, and they were long dead. There was something soothing about working around the kitchen, cooking and cleaning up. Haven didn't know what it was, but he wanted to enjoy it while he could. It wouldn't last long.

He kept an eye on Dimitri as he worked. Luckily, Dimitri seemed to have gotten the message, and he stayed in his chair. Haven continued watching him every so often. He felt vulnerable after talking to Dimitri and the moment they'd shared, and he had to get out of his funk.

It wasn't a good idea, but Haven couldn't help but feel close to Dimitri. He needed to check Dimitri's wound again, and that would undoubtedly help him put some distance between them. If he could act as Dimitri's doctor, everything would be fine.

Hopefully. *Maybe.*

Haven tried to convince himself of that as he finished cleaning up the kitchen. He kept glancing at Dimitri, but Dimitri wasn't looking at him. He was lost in his thoughts, and that was more than okay with Haven. He doubted Dimitri shared his feelings. Hell, he didn't even know what those feelings were. Dimitri was turning him upside down, and he didn't like it. It *had* to be something only he felt, though. It didn't matter that Dimitri had touched his cheek or taken his hand the day before. The circumstances called for a bit of closeness, and Dimitri no doubt wanted that.

Haven wasn't sure he could give it to him. He had to keep his distance from Dimitri before he did something stupid like deciding they might be able to be together.

He shook himself and finished cleaning the kitchen. Once he was done, he turned his attention back to Dimitri, knowing that if he didn't, his thoughts would get lost again. "I want to look at your wound."

Dimitri blinked. "I can do it on my own."

"The fact that you can doesn't mean you should have to do it. I'm still with you for now. Let me do it for you."

He expected Dimitri to argue, but to his surprise, Dimitri nodded and got to his feet. This time, when he tried to walk, his expression was steadier. Haven didn't miss the way he gritted his teeth, but they managed to get to the bathroom, and Dimitri sat on the closed toilet. Then he got back to his feet.

Haven had noticed Dimitri had found the cache of new clothes in the bathroom, and they were both dressed similarly. He made sure not to stare as Dimitri pushed the sweatpants he was wearing down his thighs, then sat again. At least he was wearing underwear. Haven wasn't sure what he would have done otherwise.

Haven gathered everything he would need, then knelt next to Dimitri. The floor was cold and hard under his knees, but he didn't move. Instead, he used it as a reminder of what was happening and what he was doing. He had to focus on Dimitri, not on how being so close to him made his stomach feel like it was filled with butterflies.

He gently unwrapped the wound, cleaned it, and poked at it for a bit. "It looks like it's healing well."

Dimitri grimaced. "I'm relieved. It feels like it's about to fall off."

Haven couldn't help but smile at that. "I think you're a bit dramatic."

"You would be too if you'd been stabbed in the thigh with a giant sword."

"Our swords aren't giant. They're calibrated to every hero."

"That sword *felt* giant when it sank into my flesh. Trust

me."

Haven laughed. "I've been wounded by swords more than once. I remember how it feels."

Dimitri peered at him. His long hair fanned across his shoulders, and Haven wanted to bury his fingers into it. "When have you been wounded by hero swords? I thought you guys worked together."

"We also train together."

"And you train by stabbing each other?"

"Of course not. But we do train with real swords, because we have to get used to their weight and how they feel. So yes, I've been a victim of stabbing several times, and I'm not the only one. You don't have to worry, though. I doubt you'll ever get stabbed again."

Dimitri wrinkled his nose, and Haven looked away because it was adorable and he didn't know if he could resist doing something stupid.

"I'm certainly not *planning* on being stabbed again," Dimitri agreed.

Haven didn't know what it was about him. Dimitri made Haven want things he shouldn't be wanting, like reaching up and cupping Dimitri's face to bring him closer and feel how soft his lips were, how his beard would feel against Haven's naked skin.

Haven managed to keep his hands under control. Instead of doing everything he wanted to do to Dimitri and more, he wrapped the wound again, then got to his feet. He washed his hands and put everything away, but then he found himself at a loss.

"What are we doing now?" Dimitri asked, apparently feeling the same way.

"I don't know. We have to wait."

"There's a TV. We can watch a movie." Dimitri sighed in pleasure. "It's been ages since I last saw a movie."

They headed back to the living room. Haven gave Dimitri space but stayed close enough that if Dimitri needed him, he would be able to help him.

Haven wasn't comfortable with how he felt. He didn't want to be attracted to Dimitri, but he couldn't deny he was. He didn't know what it meant for either of them, and he wasn't sure he would get to find out.

He also wasn't sure whether or not finding out would be a good or bad thing.

Haven was nervous, and Dimitri wasn't sure why. Was it because of the moment they'd shared earlier? Nothing had happened, which was both a pity and a relief. Now wasn't the moment to get into a relationship or even only sex, and Haven was the worst person Dimitri could do this with. He'd been very clear — he'd leave. He would go back to the conclave, and once he was with them again, either he would be killed, or he would get back in the ranks and start doing what the conclave wanted again.

Because Dimitri had no doubt that would happen — no matter how much Haven wanted to believe the conclave would listen to him, they wouldn't. Dimitri had been trying to explain what he did and why for centuries, and they still thought they should kill him. But maybe Haven would manage to get through to them. He was a hero after all, and heroes were the lifeblood of the conclave. If there was someone who could convince them they should check on the supernatural creatures they wanted to kill before they did, it was him.

Dimitri didn't want him to try, though.

No matter how much he hoped, things wouldn't end well for Haven. The conclave wouldn't listen. That much, Dimitri was sure of. It meant they would kill Haven, which was one more reason for Dimitri to stay away from him. He couldn't lose someone he loved again, which was the reason he stayed away from love. He didn't have relationships, not often. He couldn't.

His last serious relationship had been with Clementine, and he'd been incredibly sad to leave her behind, even though he'd done the right thing. Now Clementine was happy. She'd married a good man, and they had two children. That was something Dimitri wouldn't have been able to give her. He couldn't have children, not when there were already so many of them who needed him out there. He couldn't have a relationship because he had to focus on the children, not on himself. A relationship with Haven was a particularly bad idea, too, so Dimitri should stop thinking about it.

He cleared his throat. "You could go back now," he said, even though it was the last thing he wanted.

Haven frowned. "What do you mean?"

"Well, I know your friend said we should wait here, but since you're not planning on coming with us anyway, you could go now and leave me alone. I can be on my own for a few hours, maybe even a few days, depending on how long it takes for your friend to get here."

Haven shook his head. "I'm not going anywhere. I told Thor I would stay with you, and I will."

Dimitri wasn't surprised. He hadn't really thought he could convince Haven to go, not in this situation. Haven felt guilty for Dimitri being wounded, and he wouldn't leave him until he was sure Dimitri was safe and in good hands. It wasn't that he didn't trust Dimitri to take care of himself. It was more that he didn't think Dimitri could do it in this situation, with a wound in his leg and not knowing where he was. And maybe he wasn't wrong. Dimitri couldn't say he was looking forward to being left alone, but he had to offer.

He was relieved Haven had brushed him off, though.

The fact that Haven seemed to think Dimitri was his

responsibility was sweet. Dimitri wasn't used to being taken care of, and it made something in his chest feel tight. He liked it. He enjoyed the sensation of someone worrying about him, wanting to make sure he was okay. He didn't need it, though.

"You'll have to go back eventually," he pointed out. "You said you don't want to leave the heroes. That means the less time you spend hiding, the better it will be for your case. I doubt you'll be able to go back to them as if nothing happened if you stay with me for weeks. As it is, it's been only a few days."

Haven shook his head. "It won't change anything. They already know I'm on the run with you, and they know I don't want to kill you. I also wounded another hero."

Dimitri frowned. "So? You wound each other during training. How is this different?" But it was, and very much so.

"He was in the line of duty. So was I. I shouldn't have fought him. I wouldn't have if he hadn't been threatening to kill you."

Dimitri could too easily imagine how things would have gone if Haven had taken the offer the other hero had made. Together, they could have killed Dimitri, and Haven would have a chance to get back into the conclave. As it was, though, no matter what Haven seemed to think, Dimitri doubted he would be allowed back. The conclave didn't take kindly to being disobeyed, and Haven had done exactly that, and more than once. It was a miracle he was still alive, and Dimitri doubted it would last for long.

"I can take care of myself," he said. "You have to think about your future and what you want. You look suspicious enough already, just like you said. You could blame everything on me, though. Maybe tell them I learned how to hypnotize people. Tell them I used my powers against you. Tell them I forced you to help me. I don't know. I'm sure you can come up with something. But if you're truly planning on going back, you should do it now."

Haven stopped in front of the couch and glared at Dimitri. "Stop that. I'm not going anywhere, no matter how many times you try to convince me. I won't leave you, so you should stop talking about it and focus on what you want to watch."

Dimitri sighed. He didn't want Haven to go back, not now, and not ever. He was sure Haven would die if he did so, and he wanted to save Haven the way Haven had saved him.

He couldn't, though. He couldn't convince Haven to stick around. They didn't have a relationship, and he wasn't sure he would have been able to even if they had. No matter what Haven had said, no matter how he felt about the situation, it was obvious he didn't want to lose the conclave. He didn't want to lose the heroes, the work he'd done over the years, the sense of belonging they gave him.

Haven had been told again and again over hundreds of years that he was a hero, that who and what he was were the same. He'd been told he had to obey the conclave because otherwise, he wouldn't be a real hero. He would be a disgrace. So Haven, just like every other hero, had worked hard to please the conclave.

Which brought them to this moment. No matter what Haven thought, he didn't want to lose his family, and Dimitri could understand it.

He could understand it, but that didn't mean he had to be happy with it. He knew Haven would die if he went back, and he didn't want that. Even if nothing happened between them, if they never got together, Haven didn't deserve to die for saving him. He didn't deserve to die, period. Haven deserved to *live*, possibly not as a hero. He deserved to have the life he wanted instead of obeying orders that shouldn't be given.

Dimitri couldn't do anything about it, though. He wished he could, but Haven was out of his reach.

The conclave knew what Haven was doing. There would be no hiding from them, not when Mather had talked to him and seen him protecting Dimitri, and worse, when Haven had talked to Marsha. He'd told her he didn't believe Dimitri should be killed. He'd asked her to change her mind.

She hadn't, or rather, she hadn't been able to. They weren't her orders. They were the conclave's, and Haven had disobeyed. There was no way he would be welcomed back with open arms, no matter how much he wanted it. He knew better. The conclave could be ruthless, especially with people they trusted who broke that trust. Haven had made a mistake, and he would pay for it. He just prayed the conclave would listen to him before doing anything.

He still hoped to change their mind, even though he realized it was probably stupid. He had to find a way to make them see Dimitri was doing the right thing, and that Haven couldn't just abandon him when he was wounded, or worse, kill him. Dimitri had done nothing that warranted being killed, and Haven would make sure it didn't happen. Haven *knew* he was doing the right thing, and nothing would stop him.

"You don't have to worry about me," he told Dimitri.

Dimitri's expression was enough to tell him it was a stupid thing to say. "Of course I worry about you. You saved me. You didn't kill me, and you didn't let the other hero hurt me. Why shouldn't I worry about you? Especially when I know what the conclave will do if you go back to them. You can't, Haven."

Dimitri wouldn't be reassured until Haven promised him he wouldn't go, but Haven couldn't promise that. He couldn't make any kind of promises other than that he would protect Dimitri as well as he could. "Don't worry about me," he repeated. "I'm not going anywhere for now. Focus on healing and on getting better."

Dimitri quirked a brow. "I thought you were doing that."

"I am, but you can contribute. I'm not sure what's going to happen when Thor gets here, but I suspect we'll have to move. Eventually, we might have to separate. Have you thought about where to go from here?"

Dimitri grimaced. "I don't think I can go to any of the places I usually travel to, not while I'm wounded. Maybe once I'm healed. In the meantime, I probably need to keep the wound clean, and that's not going to happen in the forest. Besides, I don't have a bed anywhere."

Haven frowned. "You didn't have a motel room when you worked with the kids?"

"I didn't. I usually sleep in the forest with the wolves or bears when I do this kind of thing. It's easier."

"Easier, but also dangerous. And like you said, you can't do that now, not without risking an infection. We have to find you a safe place where you can stay until you heal."

"I want to stay with you."

It was the first time Dimitri said that plainly, and Haven didn't know how to answer him. He wanted to tell him he wanted to stay with him, too, but he couldn't. He couldn't make himself vulnerable. He couldn't allow Dimitri to know how he felt, how he might feel if they had more time, and if he allowed himself to fall in love.

He cleared his throat and gestured behind himself. "I need to call Thor. I want to see where he is."

Dimitri's expression told him how he felt about that. "Why do you need to call him?"

"Because I want to find out when he'll be here. We can hunker down in this cave for a bit, but the food will eventually be gone, as will the supplies I need for your wound and the meds."

"I'm sure he knows that, since he was the one to tell us to

come here. You're worrying for nothing, Haven."

He wasn't wrong, and Haven *was* worrying for nothing, at least when it came to this. He was also worried about a long list of other things, and he didn't know how to deal with it.

He worried about what was going to be next for Dimitri, whether or not he would leave when Haven told him to. He worried about the feelings he was starting to develop for Dimitri. He worried about how Dimitri felt about him, and of course, about the conclave. He worried he'd lost his life and that nothing he could do would get it back.

Worst of all, he didn't know what to do. It wasn't like him, but there was *nothing* he could do right now. He was always proactive, always taking the next step to ensure that whatever was happening, it yielded the result he wanted. He couldn't in this case, though.

He left Dimitri in the kitchen and headed toward the weapons room, which, along with the bathroom, were the only rooms in which he could get some privacy. He didn't think Thor would say anything Dimitri shouldn't hear, but just in case, he wanted to make sure he was alone when he called.

Thor answered after only a few rings. "Don't tell me you already killed him," he said.

Haven almost snapped, but even though he didn't know Thor well, he could hear the hint of teasing in his voice. "I haven't. We haven't been alone in this cave for a long time, though."

Thor laughed. "You're right. Give it a few more days, and you might want to strangle him. I'll be there before that happens, though. In fact, we'll arrive tomorrow."

Haven was both relieved and sorry about that. "That was fast."

"It has to be fast. I've heard some things about your man."

"He's not my man."

"If you say so. But from what I know, the conclave has been

trying to find him for hundreds of years. He's eluded them until now, and they're angry that he continues doing so, and worst of all, he's managed to convince one of their best heroes to help him. They're not happy, Haven. I don't think they'll welcome you back, whatever you say."

Haven was aware of that, and he didn't want to talk about it more than he already had. "Is there anything I can do in the meantime?"

"Just stay in the cave, maybe check the cameras, although I doubt the conclave can find you there. Tryg is very particular when it comes to his caves, and ever since he met Isaac, he's even more careful with security. Nothing will happen to you, not until we get there. Then we'll talk and decide what the next step is, both for you and your man."

Haven didn't protest Thor's choice of words. He knew Thor had heard him the first time, and he was doing it on purpose. He probably wanted to get a rise out of Haven, and he might have in other circumstances.

Haven didn't mind Dimitri being called his man, though. He had to be careful, because nothing could happen between them, but it was a nice dream.

A dream he could have for the next few days, or maybe only until tomorrow. If today was the last day he'd have with Dimitri, maybe he should make the most out of it. He knew nothing should happen between them, because it would make it harder for both of them to take a step back, but they could talk. They could be friends, at least for today.

CHAPTER TEN

When it was time to go to bed, Dimitri couldn't stop staring at the bed. He hadn't thought about it until now, but now that he did, he realized Haven hadn't slept with him last night. He couldn't even remember falling asleep, which was normal, considering he was wounded. He suspected Haven had slept on the floor, or maybe on the small couch, and neither would have been comfortable. It made sense, though. Haven was a bit of a mother hen with Dimitri, making sure he wasn't in pain and that he had everything he needed, and since Dimitri was wounded, Haven would have wanted him to have as much space as he could.

Dimitri was much better now, though, and even though he was still reliant on painkillers, he didn't want Haven to spend a second night on the floor. It wasn't right, especially not with everything Haven was doing for him. He should be able to spend the night in a bed, and since there was only one of them, they would have to share.

It had been a long time since Dimitri had shared a bed with anyone.

He settled under the blankets, watching Haven as he moved around the small cave. When Haven stepped toward the couch, Dimitri knew he was right. That was where Haven had spent last night, and where he was apparently going to spend tonight, too. Considering how tall Haven was, his legs had to dangle from one side of the couch. There was no way it was comfortable or that Haven would be able to get much sleep, and Dimitri had to take the next step. Did it matter that there was only one bed? They were both adults, and they could share without a problem.

Or at least, Dimitri hoped so.

He was aware of his feelings for Haven, of how much they were growing, and of the fact that Haven didn't feel the same way. That didn't mean they couldn't sleep in the same bed, though. Dimitri could keep his hands to himself. He might wrap himself around Haven during the night, but he suspected Haven wouldn't say anything. He would slip out of bed before Dimitri realized what was happening, and he would never mention it. That was just the kind of man he was.

Dimitri cleared his throat.

Haven looked at him right away, frowning. "What's going on? Are you in pain? Did you take your painkillers?"

Dimitri smiled. Haven was worried about him, and it made him feel better. It probably shouldn't, but he liked the thought that someone cared, that someone wanted him to be okay. He liked that *Haven* cared. "You slept on the couch last night?"

Haven looked down and grimaced. "I did. But don't worry. I've slept in less comfortable places."

"I don't doubt that, but I don't understand why you should when there's a perfectly good bed we can share."

"You're still healing."

Dimitri stared at Haven, wondering if that was all there was to it. Maybe he wasn't comfortable. Maybe he could tell Dimitri was attracted to him, and he wanted to stay away. It would be understandable. "I won't do anything," he promised. "I'll keep my hands to myself, and I won't suggest we do anything we shouldn't do."

Haven blinked. "What are you talking about? I'm afraid I'll hurt you if I move during the night."

Dimitri relaxed. "You won't. I promise. This bed is big enough that we don't even have to touch during the night." Dimitri couldn't deny he hoped it would happen, but there really was enough space they could each stay on their side of the bed and not come in contact. "Come on. What if something happens? What if someone attacks us? Can you fight with a backache?"

They both knew he was right, but Haven still hesitated. Eventually, though, he took a step toward the bed. Dimitri grinned at him and patted the spot next to him, but when Haven slipped under the blankets, Dimitri moved to the side more so they wouldn't touch. He lay down, pressing his head against his pillow, feeling how tense Haven was even though they weren't touching. He wanted to help, but he wasn't sure how. Why was Haven tense? Was he worried someone would attack while he slept? Or was he worried that he would hurt Dimitri? Was it something else?

Dimitri didn't know, but he doubted Haven would be able to sleep until he relaxed.

He turned to his side so he could face Haven's back and almost laughed. Haven had pushed himself to the very edge of the mattress, so much so that Dimitri expected him to fall on his face at any second. It didn't surprise him, though. If the main reason Haven hadn't slept with him last night was that he didn't want to jostle his wound, he would make sure he stayed as far away from Dimitri as he could.

Before he thought too much about it, Dimitri reached out and touched Haven's back. Haven went ramrod straight, but he didn't turn to look at Dimitri.

"You need to relax," Dimitri murmured.

"I don't know if I can," Haven admitted.

There was so much vulnerability in his voice that Dimitri's chest squeezed painfully.

Haven wasn't vulnerable. He was strong, capable, always knew what to do, or at least, it was an exterior he tried very hard to portray. But he was allowing Dimitri to see him as he really was, and it touched Dimitri probably more than it should. "We're both adults," Dimitri started.

Haven finally turned around to face him. "That's not what I'm worried about. I'm worried about your wound. I don't want to hurt you, even by accident."

"You won't. I know you. You wouldn't hurt me even if you were asleep. I *trust* you." Dimitri hesitated. If he wanted Haven to feel comfortable, he should probably be honest. "And while it's true that I'm attracted to you and that I like you, I promise you I won't touch you in any way you don't want. I can keep my hands to myself. You don't have to worry about that."

Haven was silent for so long that Dimitri wondered if he'd done the right thing. He'd thought that if he wanted Haven to be honest with him, he would have to be honest with Haven, he had to admit how he felt. He could have been wrong. But they were sharing a bed, and it was the least he could do. Hopefully, it would help Haven relax. Dimitri couldn't do much more than promising him he wouldn't touch him, and he hoped it would be enough.

"Why?" Haven asked.

Dimitri blinked, wondering what he was asking. "Why what?"

"Why won't you try anything?"

Dimitri bit his lower lip. "Well, I thought it was obvious. To begin with, I don't know if you're attracted to me. But you're also a hero, and eventually, you'll leave. I don't want to give you my heart if you're going to take it away from me."

Haven fell silent again, and to Dimitri's surprise, he moved closer. Dimitri stayed still, wondering what was happening. Maybe Haven was finally relaxing. That was what Dimitri had wanted to happen, so he relaxed, too.

At least until Haven reached for him.

Before he could say anything, he found himself dragged closer. His thigh twinged, but it only lasted a few seconds, because then Haven's lips landed on his.

Dimitri sucked in a breath. He didn't know what was happening, not beyond the fact that Haven was kissing him and that he wanted to make the most out of it. He didn't know if it would happen again, but he suspected that even if it did, it would stay physical, and only that. Neither of them could afford anything more to happen.

They could afford a kiss, though.

It was madness, but that wouldn't stop Haven. He'd wanted to do this for a while, almost since the first moment he'd met Dimitri, and now, he was.

He knew they should talk. Like Dimitri had said, Haven was a hero, while Dimitri was a supernatural creature. Haven was planning to leave, and they probably wouldn't see each other again. They shouldn't be doing this, but Haven couldn't find it in himself to care about all the reasons why. He wanted Dimitri. He wanted to feel close to him, to feel his skin against his, his mouth on him. Right now, there was nothing he wanted more, and he couldn't stop.

He continued kissing Dimitri, wondering what was next. He didn't know what Dimitri wanted, and he didn't want to push.

Dimitri wasn't shy about making what he wanted known, though. He pushed his hands under Haven's t-shirt, pulling and tugging until Haven finally got the message and allowed him to pull it off. When Haven moved back toward him, they stared at each other for a while. Dimitri opened his mouth, maybe to ask what they were doing, if they really should be doing this, but Haven didn't want him to think about it. They'd have time for regret later. Right now, they should focus on each other.

He kissed Dimitri again. He never stopped thinking about

the wound on Dimitri's thigh, knowing he had to be careful and ready to move away if he had to. Dimitri didn't seem to care as much, and Haven caught him wincing a few times as they moved. When Dimitri rolled to his back and pulled Haven along with him, Haven was careful to lean his weight against Dimitri's other thigh. He didn't know if this was the only time they'd do this, but he wanted Dimitri to enjoy it as much as he would.

Dimitri buried his hands into Haven's hair, pulling him closer. He also tried to wiggle out of his borrowed sweatpants as he did so, and they found themselves tangled, their legs twined together. Dimitri chuckled against Haven's lips, and Haven took the opportunity to kiss a path down Dimitri's neck.

Dimitri groaned and opened his legs even more. Haven could feel him through their sweatpants, hard and pushing forward as if seeking more contact. And maybe he was. Haven certainly felt like he couldn't get enough of Dimitri right now.

Dimitri's beard was strange under Haven's touch, but not in a bad way. It felt like fresh grass under Haven's feet— something Haven hadn't felt in too long. He buried his hands in Dimitri's hair, gently tugging until he had Dimitri in the position he wanted him in.

Dimitri didn't protest, watching Haven, his eyes wide and sparkling in the soft light that came from the kitchen.

They both wanted this. Hell, if Haven could have his way, he wanted much more than this.

He wanted a life for himself, a life in which he wouldn't have to obey orders, a life he could choose how to live.

But he couldn't have that. He was a hero. He'd been born a hero, and he would die a hero. No matter how many times he wished things would be different, he knew they weren't. He had to make the most out of this moment, and he would.

He was careful as he tugged off Dimitri's t-shirt and his pants. He had borrowed a pair of clean underwear, too, and Haven slid those down his legs as well.

The t-shirt got tangled in Dimitri's horns a few times, and Haven found himself wishing he had the time to learn how to move around them. He wondered how it would feel to have Dimitri suck him off while he held onto those horns.

He wondered many things, but he didn't have time to do all of them.

Once Dimitri was naked, Haven watched him. Dimitri didn't seem to be ashamed of his body, and he didn't have a reason to be. He was slender, tall, and his skin was so pale that it reflected the light coming from the kitchen. He opened his arms, but Haven didn't lean back into them, not yet. Instead, he kissed down Dimitri's stomach, stopping to tease his bellybutton, looking up to make sure that what he was doing was welcome.

Dimitri's eyes were hooded, and he stared down with wonder, as if what they were doing was the oddest thing he'd ever seen.

That was the case for Haven. He doubted he would ever be able to have sex again without thinking about this moment, and that was okay. He would carry the memories for a long time, and since he was immortal, Dimitri would always be with him.

He hovered over Dimitri's cock, the moment feeling as if it would make or break everything. If Haven changed his mind, he could go back up, kiss Dimitri again and make sure he came as they rutted against each other. If he went down, though, he would suck Dimitri's cock, and he suspected Dimitri's flavor would stay with him forever. It would make it impossible to forget Dimitri, right along with everything else Dimitri was and did.

Haven had to take that chance, though.

He wrapped his lips around the head of Dimitri's cock, half-smiling when Dimitri's hips shot up. He didn't have to ask to know if Dimitri liked this. That meant he didn't have to stop, and he was more than happy not to.

He focused, wanting to bring as much pleasure as possible to Dimitri. It had been a while since he'd done this, but he was more than happy to do it. He had to lay down on his stomach, placing himself between Dimitri's thighs, making sure Dimitri didn't move too much because of the wound. It was hard, especially when Dimitri started writhing under him as he sucked, so Haven used his arms and hands to keep Dimitri in place.

The movement, or maybe feeling pinned under him, made Dimitri wriggle even harder, and his moans became louder. He reached down, burying his fingers into Haven's hair, pulling him up, then pushing him down to the point that Haven wasn't sure what Dimitri wanted. He continued sucking until Dimitri pulled so hard that it hurt. Then, he let go of Dimitri's cock with a pop and looked up. "What's wrong?"

Dimitri shook his head. His cheeks were flushed, and while Haven shouldn't have been surprised to see that the color was a light blue instead of pink, he was. It was another alien sight, but he was endearing and beautiful.

"I want you to come up here. I want us to come together, or at least to work toward it together. I feel like you're taking care of me, but I'm not doing anything for you."

Haven shook his head. "I'm fine. I can continue."

"I want you to come up here, though."

Haven didn't ask if he was sure. He climbed on top of Dimitri again, and this time, he ditched his sweatpants. He abandoned them between the sheets, careful of the way he was placing himself on top of Dimitri's body. He didn't miss the way Dimitri rolled his eyes, but that was fine. Haven was always going to make sure Dimitri was okay and to take care of him, even when Dimitri thought it was overkill.

The sensation of naked skin against naked skin was maddening. Dimitri wrapped his good leg around Haven's body, holding him close as he moved under him. Haven couldn't say he minded the position. He would have been more than happy to continue sucking Dimitri off, but instead, they would both be coming, and it would be glorious. Everything Dimitri did was, and the sex wasn't any different.

They rutted against each other, Haven the more controlled one, Dimitri with abandon. Still, when Dimitri came between them, it took all Haven had not to come, too. Instead, he continued moving, slowing down so it wouldn't be overwhelming for Dimitri.

He should have known better.

Dimitri's eyes popped open. Then he grabbed Haven's ass with both hands, pulling him close. "Come on. I want you to come, too."

He didn't have to say it twice. Haven felt like he was about to explode, and he wanted to come desperately.

His dick slotted in the groove between Dimitri's groin and his leg, and Haven thrust against him until he, too, came. He screwed his eyes shut, surrendering to the pleasure and wondering if he could have this again. He wanted to, but there was no way for either of them to know what the future would be like. It didn't look good for them to have anything more.

Right now, though, Haven found himself wondering if it was at all possible, and he found himself wishing. He wanted Dimitri, and Dimitri wanted him.

Was that such a bad thing?

CHAPTER ELEVEN

Dimitri woke up to the feeling that someone was watching him. He smiled, thinking it was Haven, but when he opened his eyes, he found Haven still asleep next to him, an arm and a leg hooked around him.

If he wasn't one watching Dimitri, who was?

Dimitri looked around, his gaze stopping on a man standing over their bed. Dimitri stayed still for a second. Then he freaked out and shifted.

He became a mouse without even thinking about it, needing to protect himself. It was selfish — he should be thinking about protecting Haven, too.

He didn't need to. The shift woke Haven up, and he jerked, looking around. Dimitri could see he started to jump out of bed only to stop and groan, then fall back against the pillow and pull the blankets up.

"When you said you would be here tomorrow, I thought it would be toward the middle of the day, or maybe the evening," he said.

"It *is* evening," the man pointed out. He peered at Dimitri, who was half-hidden under the pillow.

"You freaked him out," Haven said, looking at Dimitri, too.

"I'm sorry. I didn't mean to, but I didn't expect to walk in on both of you naked and wrapped around each other."

Haven huffed and reached out for Dimitri, and Dimitri allowed him to take him. He didn't want this man to see Haven naked, but he realized there was nothing he could do about that. Besides, he shouldn't feel protective or proprietary about

Haven. Haven wasn't his to protect.

Haven wrapped the sheet around his body, then got to his feet. His eyes widened when he noticed there were more people in the cave, and he briefly closed his eyes, shaking his head. "Of course you're not alone. I should have realized."

"You should have, yes. Did you really think Tryg was going to allow you to use his cave without checking in on it?"

"It's a cave. What did he think I was going to do to it?"

"Well, I didn't think you were going to have sex in my bed," one of the other men said. He had to be Tryg.

Haven glared at him. Thankfully, though, he didn't say anything. Instead, he ignored everyone and carried Dimitri to the bathroom. Dimitri waited until they were there to shift back to his mostly human form and ask, "I'm guessing that was Thor?"

"You're guessing right." Haven rubbed his face. "We overslept."

He sounded surprised, and Dimitri realized he probably was. He doubted the conclave allowed heroes to oversleep, or even to rest more than a few hours if they could avoid it. Heroes were at the conclave's beck and call, and they had to obey orders, even if it meant they didn't get enough sleep.

"We should probably go back," he murmured. He wanted to take care of Haven—to make sure he got enough sleep and food. He couldn't, though, and it was easier for him to focus on what was next.

He didn't know if Haven would come with them, but he hoped so. If Haven went back to the conclave, he would die, and Dimitri didn't want that to happen. He couldn't imagine a life in which Haven wasn't alive. If he had to live without Haven, he could. He'd been alone for a long time, and he was used to it. He didn't want to think about Haven being dead, though. It was horrifying, and it almost made him freak out again.

To his surprise, Haven cupped his cheek and kissed his forehead. "Relax. I promise they won't hurt you. They might be teasing and huffy, but they're good people."

That was all Dimitri needed to trust them. If Haven did, so did he.

They quickly showered. Once they were dressed, they went back to the main room. Someone had made coffee, and the four men were gathered around the island, sipping on steaming mugs. Two of them were sitting down, and Dimitri's eyes widened when he noticed that one had red eyes. The red-eyed man winked, then offered Dimitri his hand. "Cecil," he said.

Dimitri shook his hand, nodding. "Dimitri."

Cecil peered at him. "A leshy, huh? I wasn't sure there were any of you guys left around."

"There are more of us than you think. What about you? A mage?"

Cecil shrugged one shoulder. "Got it in one. although I guess the red eyes are a dead giveaway."

Dimitri nodded, then turned to the other sitting man. He reached for him, intent on shaking his hand, but Tryg growled. Dimitri froze, wondering what was going on. The smaller man rolled his eyes then took Dimitri's hand in his. "I'm Isaac. Ignore him. He's overprotective."

"I didn't say anything," Tryg protested.

"You didn't have to. You scared him by growling." Isaac looked at him like he'd hung the moon.

Dimitri didn't have to ask to know those two were together.

The only one left was Thor. Dimitri looked at the man, wondering why Thor had decided to help Haven after what had gone down between them. Sure, Haven hadn't killed him, but he was still a hero.

Of course, Dimitri had done the same. He'd trusted Haven

way too early, especially considering how distrustful he usually was.

"Well, you two look better when you're dressed," Thor teased. He shook Dimitri's hand, then tilted his chin toward Dimitri's thigh. "I hope you weren't too vigorous last night considering you're wounded."

Haven put his hands on Dimitri's shoulders and pulled him back, closer to him and away from Thor. "None of your business," he snapped.

Thor crossed his arms over his chest. "You're right. What you do in your private life is none of my business. I'd like to know what's going on, though."

Haven didn't seem to want to explain. Still, his hands relaxed on Dimitri's shoulders. "As you can see, Dimitri is a leshy. The conclave wanted me to kill him, and I decided I didn't want to. We both ran. I hope I can still go back, but Dimitri needs a safe place to hide, especially while he's healing."

Thor looked at both of them, then nodded. "We can do that."

Haven relaxed even more. He kissed the top of Dimitri's head, surprising everyone, probably including himself, and turned to Cecil. "How are you feeling?"

Cecil blinked at him. "I'm not sure what you're asking."

"Well, you lost your brother. It couldn't have been easy."

"I'll be fine. It hurt more to lose one of my best friends, but thanks for asking." He looked at Thor, and Dimitri could tell they were together, too. There was so much love in Cecil's gaze, and it made Dimitri's heart ache and long for a love of his own. "I doubt I would be feeling this well if I didn't have Thor, and of course, Tryg and Isaac. That, and I don't have to keep on running from Fabrice."

Thor smiled at him and took his hand. "We should sit down and talk," he told Haven.

Haven stepped away from Dimitri, and Dimitri missed him already. He couldn't deny his presence was critical in this conversation, though.

Even though Cecil wasn't human, Haven cared about his well-being. He might be a hero, but that wasn't all he was. He was also human and caring, and Dimitri found himself hoping that whatever happened next, they would be able to get through it — *together*.

Haven had never thought this would happen or that he had it in him, but he wasn't against begging for help when it came to helping Dimitri. Still, he was relieved when he didn't have to. Whatever Thor had seen in him, whatever he thought, it seemed to be for Dimitri's benefit.

It was a relief. It was everything Haven had wanted over the past few days, and he was finally getting it.

"I agree he has to hide for at least a while," Thor said.

"I think that's why they called us," Tryg pointed out.

Thor rolled his eyes, but he kept his focus on Haven and Dimitri. "The conclave isn't easy to deal with," he told Dimitri.

Dimitri snorted. "I've been tangling with the conclave for centuries. I know exactly who they are and how they behave. The only reason I'm still around is that I'm wounded. If I weren't, I would have left, and they wouldn't be able to find me." He hesitated. "And of course, there's Haven." Thor's attention went back to Haven.

There was pity in his gaze, and Haven hated that. He didn't want people to pity him. There was nothing to pity him for.

"They won't welcome you back," he said.

Haven was aware of that. "Maybe not welcome me, but if I want the conclave and the heroes to change, I'm going to have to take the first step. They won't stop hurting supernatural creatures until they learn that they shouldn't."

"They already know," Dimitri murmured.

Haven ignored him. He was right, and Haven knew he would probably die for nothing, but he couldn't think about that right now. His main concern was Dimitri and making sure he was safe, and that was what Haven would do.

He left Dimitri with the others and went to pour himself a cup of coffee. He got one for Dimitri, too, and when he came back, he found the small group was talking about what was next. They had to plan, and they had to do it now. Even though they were safe in this cave, they couldn't stay for much longer.

"I think we should all move together," Thor said.

"I already told you I need to go back to the conclave," Haven intervened. He handed one of the mugs to Dimitri, who took it with a grateful smile.

Thor was still staring at them, but Haven was doing his best to ignore it. Thor finally nodded. "All right. Let's say that you really do have to go back to the conclave," he said. "You're going to be killed for it."

"Maybe. Maybe I'll be able to talk to them. They won't just kill me. They can't. I'm a hero, and I have to answer for what I did. They'll put me on trial, and it will be my chance to talk about what happened and why I did what I did. It will be the only chance to make them see that supernatural creatures aren't evil just because of what they are."

Thor shook his head. "You have more faith in them than I do, although I suppose that's normal. Going back isn't a good idea, though. Like you said, they won't welcome you. What happens after the trial? Will they let you go?"

"Maybe." And only if Haven managed to convince them he'd done the right thing by letting Dimitri go and wounding Mather. He doubted it, though. Even if he did manage to convince them to be more careful when they gave their orders, they'd still have to punish him. It was how things went.

"Maybe you can make up a story," Isaac said, voice soft. "We can come up with something they can believe so they won't kill you."

Haven highly doubted that would happen, but he still smiled at Isaac, who was too gentle for his own good. "I don't think they'll believe anything that comes out of my mouth, to be honest."

"Then how do you expect to convince them they shouldn't kill supernatural creatures?"

Haven stared at him, wondering how he could have missed that. "I'll find a way. I'll explain what Dimitri was doing and why, and I'm sure they'll realize the children need to be protected. Dimitri is helping us, not working against us." Because after all, heroes were born to protect humanity, not to kill supernatural creatures just because of what they were.

"I want you to come with us," Dimitri said quietly. He wasn't looking at Haven, but he didn't have to for Haven to know how he was feeling. "I know you want to go back," he continued. "And I won't be able to stop you if that's what you want. But please. Give us some time to come up with a story, or at least, with a plan to help you. The conclave won't listen to you, no matter what you think. You're only going back to get killed, and I don't want that to happen."

Haven reached for him, taking one of his hands and squeezing. "I'll be fine, and I'll be coming with you, at least for now."

"I don't like that *for now*," Dimitri said with a self-deprecating smile. "But fine. We can table this conversation."

"Thank the Gods," Tryg muttered. Haven glared at him. Tryg glared right back. "We should go. We haven't been found yet, but it can't last forever. How are we traveling? Smoke?"

"I'll open a portal," Haven said.

"Can't the conclave control those and follow you through them?"

Haven wasn't surprised Tryg knew about it. He would have wanted to know that kind of thing, too, if the conclave was after him. "I can make a portal the conclave won't know about. Don't worry. I don't want them to find Dimitri, and I'll do everything I can to make sure they don't." Even if it was the last thing he did—even if it killed him. Dimitri would be safe—even if Haven had to give his life for it.

Dimitri would miss the cave. He wasn't sure if it was because of what the place meant for him and Haven or because it had made him feel safe in a moment in which he hadn't thought anything could. Whatever the reason, he hoped that eventually, he and Haven could go back. In the meantime, they would stay in Thor's apartment, and apparently, they would stay with Thor and Cecil, as well as Tryg and Isaac.

Dimitri wasn't sure how that would work. He didn't stay with people. He only stayed with his wolves or bears, and he knew how to behave with them. People were different.

He wasn't antisocial. He didn't mind talking to people or even being close to them, but he didn't often have the opportunity to do that. In his line of work, the only people he talked to were the children and the people who helped them, and even that didn't last long. His closest friend was Clementine, and they weren't friends. They hadn't been in a long time. She'd been happy to see him again, but she had her own life, and Dimitri wasn't going to fuck that up for her.

So no, he didn't have any friends, and he wasn't sure how to behave with the four men who were helping him. He'd thanked them several times already, but they'd brushed it off every single time. He didn't know what else to do.

"As long as you stay away from my bedroom and the one

Tryg and Isaac are using, you can go anywhere you want in the apartment," Thor said as he showed Dimitri and Haven the place. "There's another guest room, but if you want to room separately, one of you can use the couch." He looked at them, no doubt wondering what their answer would be.

He seemed to be especially curious about what was happening between Dimitri and Haven, and Dimitri didn't blame him. He was curious, too. He and Haven were incredibly different, and he didn't know if anything would come out of whatever they were doing, but he found himself hoping. Yes, he was a supernatural creature, a leshy, while Haven was a hero. Did that mean they couldn't be together? As long as Haven didn't go back to the conclave, Dimitri didn't think there was a reason for them to stay away from each other.

But Haven was going back, wasn't he?

Dimitri still hoped he could change Haven's mind. Haven seemed convinced, but he'd given in. He was still with Dimitri, and he'd told Dimitri he'd stick with him for a while. Hopefully, that would give Dimitri time to make him see that going back to the conclave was rash and stupid. The conclave would never understand. Dimitri should know—he'd been trying to convince them for hundreds of years. Haven was the first hero who'd stopped and listened to him, and Dimitri didn't want to lose that.

He didn't want to lose Haven.

He was lonely. He loved his animals, and he loved the children he saved, but it wasn't the same. It didn't replace having a friend, a relationship, someone to love who would love him in return. He'd never thought he wanted that, but now, watching Cecil and Thor, and Isaac and Tryg, he found himself wondering. Could he and Haven have that? It would be hard, but what relationship wasn't? The fact that they were different didn't mean they couldn't be together, and from the way Haven was behaving, Dimitri wondered if maybe he wanted the same. There was no way for Dimitri to find out until they talked, though, and for now, he wasn't planning on doing that.

"We can stay together," Haven said gruffly.

Thor grinned. "That's what I thought. All right, then." He pushed open a door. "You'll stay here. I don't know how long we'll hang around here, but you're safe. I doubt the conclave would think to look for you here even if they knew about this place. They attempted to find Tryg and me for a while, and we know all the tricks to keep them away. You can lay low for a bit, and then we'll talk again."

Dimitri swallowed as he stepped into the bedroom. It wasn't huge, but it was vastly different from what he was used to. Of course, he was used to the forest, so everything was different. It wasn't the cave, but it was a private space, a space he would share with Haven. He didn't know what it meant, but he couldn't wait to find out.

The door closed, making him jerk. He turned around to see that Thor was gone, while Haven was standing there, looking around.

They didn't have anything with them, but Thor had promised to make sure they had clothes and everything else they needed. There were toiletries in the attached bathroom, so they were set for a bit.

Dimitri looked around again. He didn't know what else to do. He wanted to talk to Haven, to step closer to him and lean against him, but he wasn't sure where they stood. They'd both apparently decided they couldn't be together yesterday. Then, they'd also decided they didn't care. What did that mean for them? What did it mean for the way they behaved with each other?

Dimitri knew he shouldn't be doing this, that it was crazy, but for once, he didn't care about that. He wanted this. He wanted this one thing for himself, to have Haven in his life. It might be stupid, but now that he'd given in, he realized that behaving as if nothing was happening would be even stupider. Even if he pushed Haven away because he wanted to protect himself, it was too late. Haven was already deep under his skin, and he wasn't going anywhere.

"How are you feeling?" Haven asked.

Dimitri shrugged. "I'm fine."

"Your thigh must be hurting you. Do you want me to look at it?"

"I'm fine," Dimitri repeated, but he secretly enjoyed this. He liked Haven taking care of him.

"Sit down. I'll check the wound. I didn't have the time to do it earlier, but we're not going anywhere again."

Dimitri rolled his eyes. Haven helped him out of his sweatpants before he sat, but, to Dimitri's dismay, he didn't touch Dimitri's underwear. That was fine. Dimitri could get rid of those on his own, and he did so, grinning at Haven.

Haven's cheeks were slightly pink as he rolled his eyes and looked away.

Dimitri wasn't ashamed of his body, and he sat back on the bed, waiting. That seemed to do the trick. Haven shook himself and focused on the wound, all business once again. Dimitri couldn't help but notice that his fingertips didn't stay on his thigh, though. They roamed as if they had their own mind, but he didn't say anything about it because it was what he wanted.

"It seems to be healing well," Haven commented.

"Yes?"

"As long as you don't do anything too strenuous that would pull on the stitches, you should be fine."

"What did you have in mind that could be strenuous?"

"I think it's more what *you* had in mind. You didn't need to take off your underwear for me to check the wound."

Dimitri took a chance and buried his fingers into Haven's

hair. "I didn't need to, but I wanted to. I want to feel your hands on me again, Haven."

He expected Haven to protest, to say that now wasn't the time, but instead, Haven leaned forward and kissed him.

Dimitri closed his eyes. He didn't know what the future held for them, but he didn't have to, not right now. Right now, he just needed to focus on this and to know how right it felt.

"What do you want?" Haven whispered as he kissed down Dimitri's chest.

Dimitri could think of too many things he wanted. Since he didn't want to scare Haven away, he focused on one, the thing he wanted the most right now. "You inside me." It had been so long since he'd allowed it to happen. He had to trust whoever he was with, and he trusted Haven.

Haven froze in the act of kissing Dimitri's nipple, or maybe licking it. "Me inside you?"

"Yes." Dimitri wasn't ashamed of wanting that, and especially so of wanting it with Haven.

"I don't have anything."

It took a moment for Dimitri to understand what Haven was talking about. When he did, he rolled to his side and reached for the drawer in the nightstand. Sure enough, when he opened it, a bottle of lube rolled toward the front. He snagged it, then settled down on his back again and held it out to Haven, who looked like it might bite him.

"How did you know it was there?" Haven asked.

Dimitri shook the bottle, smiling when Haven finally took it as he leaned back on his knees. "It's just like Thor to make sure there's lube in every room of this apartment."

Haven stopped moving again. "Do you think he and Cecil used it?"

"Can we focus on what we're doing and not think about what Thor and Cecil might have done?" Not that it wouldn't be sexy as hell, but Dimitri wanted this moment to be about him and Haven, and only them.

Haven's cheeks pinked. "Of course." He opened the lube. He still looked uncertain, and Dimitri didn't like it.

"We can do something else if you'd rather," he said. He wasn't about to push Haven into something he didn't want. He wouldn't do that to anyone.

Haven shook his head. "I want it. I'm just . . . you have a lot of trust in me. I didn't expect it."

He probably hadn't, although Dimitri wasn't sure how he could have missed it. "Of course I trust you."

"I know. I don't understand why, but I know."

"You don't have to understand. You just have to be aware of it." Dimitri could tell this conversation would derail their trajectory toward pleasure, and he wasn't ready to have it. He couldn't explain even to himself why he trusted Haven so much.

He opened his legs wide and stared at Haven, who seemed to shake himself. He slathered his fingers with lube, his cock twitching as he did so, and finally reached for Dimitri.

Dimitri sighed in pleasure and closed his eyes. He loved this, and he especially loved it with Haven. Strong fingers prodded at him while warm lips closed around his cock, and he stopped thinking. He hoped Haven had finally realized Dimitri truly wanted this, because Dimitri didn't think he'd be able to speak right now.

Haven was driving him crazy, and Dimitri didn't care.

He forgot everything that wasn't what Haven was doing to him, even the pain in his thigh. Haven was careful but steady, slow but firm, and it was what Dimitri had wanted and needed.

He didn't know how much time passed, how many times his pleasure almost peaked only to recede when Haven stopped moving, but his head felt like it was about to explode, and it wasn't the only thing. Dimitri *had* to open his eyes, and the sight in front of him would have brought him to his knees if he'd been standing.

Haven was on his stomach between Dimitri's legs, his mouth around Dimitri's cock, his fingers moving in and out.

Dimitri couldn't take it anymore. He groaned and reached for Haven, and thankfully, Haven didn't ask him what he wanted. Instead, he stood on his knees, lubed his cock, and moved until he was pressed on top of Dimitri.

It was Heaven and Hell, but only for a moment. Then Haven pushed inside Dimitri, and Dimitri screwed his eyes shut. He clutched at Haven's shoulders, needing him closer, and wrapped his legs around him. They were one, and Dimitri hoped they would be for a long time.

He forgot all about that—and everything that wasn't Haven's body and how he felt against and inside him—when Haven moved. He thrust inside Dimitri, while Dimitri could only hold on for the ride.

And what a ride it was. Maybe it was because it had been so long since Dimitri had done this, or maybe it was because he was doing it with Haven. Whatever the reason, Dimitri was already about to come. He bit his lower lip to the point of pain, but Haven noticed, and he kissed him, pulling the lip away from Dimitri's teeth.

"Let go," he murmured breathlessly.

Dimitri obeyed. He wanted to, and he hoped Haven was as close to release as he was. The pleasure coiled in his groin and pushed him to the edge. He grabbed the back of Haven's head with one hand and kissed Haven, crying out against his lips when he came, pleasure flooding him and making it impossible to think or do anything except allow it to take over.

Haven grunted but didn't stop moving. He panted against Dimitri's mouth, a sign he was about to come, too. Dimitri grinned and tightened his ass, then released and tightened again. Haven's eyes widened, then he closed them and threw his head back. Dimitri clung to him as he came, the after-shocks of pleasure still echoing through him.

Then he flopped on his back. Haven stayed inside him for a bit, breathing hard, while Dimitri stroked every inch of skin he could get to. Haven deserved to be taken care of, too, and Dimitri wanted to be the one to do that.

The sound of someone clapping their hands made Haven jerk. He glared at the door, and Dimitri couldn't help but laugh as he tried to pull Haven down to the bed. "You knew Thor was going to tease you," he pointed out.

Haven relaxed, wrapping an arm around Dimitri, and pulling him close. "I knew."

"Yet, you did it anyway."

"And I don't regret it."

Dimitri didn't, either.

Haven didn't want this to end, and for the first time since he'd met Dimitri, he allowed himself to think that it didn't have to.

He and Dimitri worked well together. It wasn't just in the bedroom, but also in life in general. They'd worked well together when they'd been running from Mather and when they'd shared the cave, even though it hadn't been for long. Haven wanted to see if they could work just as well in an or-dinary life, if they could be a couple the way Thor and Cecil were. He wanted to think they could, but it was way too soon. Still, the thoughts were there, and being with Dimitri had made him realize he wasn't as alone as he'd thought. Even without the conclave, he had people he could trust, maybe even love, in Dimitri's case.

Not just Dimitri had fallen into Haven's life. Because of what was happening, Haven had had to contact Thor, and he had to trust him. He found that he didn't mind. He truly be-lieved Thor was doing this to help them, or rather, to help

Dimitri. Thor didn't resent Haven for what had happened with Cecil and Fabrice, and while Haven had a hard time believing that, he couldn't deny it. He also couldn't deny that Thor seemed to be friendly toward him, and it was easy to imagine a future in which they could be friends.

Because Haven didn't have friends.

He'd never realized how lonely the hero life was before, but now he did. Even when he worked with a hero or when he trained with them, it wasn't the same. They were never friends, only coworkers. They *couldn't* be friends. The conclave didn't want them to be. They didn't want to lose the control they had over them, and allowing them to have relationships might make that happen. What if two heroes fell in love? What if they became best friends? Their devotion wouldn't be to the conclave anymore, but to each other, and that would mean the conclave had lost them. They might not obey blind orders anymore, just like Haven wasn't.

Haven understood the reason behind the rule that heroes couldn't have relationships. He'd thought it was because they had to be focused on their job, but now, he could see the truth.

The conclave didn't want to lose the heroes, and it made sense.

Haven might know what was going on, but he had no clue what to do with it. He wanted to give himself and Dimitri a chance, but he didn't know if it could work.

He deserved it, though. After everything he'd done for the conclave, after the hundreds of years he'd worked for them, after agreeing to lose his human life to become the armed hand of the conclave, he wanted more. He wanted more than death and hunting, more than obeying orders. He wanted a life, maybe not the life he would have had if he'd stayed human, but a life nonetheless. He wasn't just a killer. He was also a man, and Dimitri had made him realize that. Dimitri had made him realize a lot of things, and Haven wanted more of that.

But if he wanted to be with Dimitri, he had to work things out. He had to find a way to make that happen. He also had to come to terms with the fact that if he did this, he'd never be able to go back. He would be on the run for the rest of his life, and since he was immortal, that would be a very long time.

It didn't matter, though. Dimitri had been on the run for a long time, as had Thor and Tryg. The conclave would kill them if they got their hands on them, but that didn't stop them from living. Hell, they were both in relationships now. They were in love, and they protected their boyfriends. Haven wanted to do that, too. He wanted to be with Dimitri, to help him save those children, to protect him from the heroes who would come. Who would do that if he didn't?

"You're thinking hard," Dimitri said, running his fingertips up and down Haven's naked chest.

Haven tightened his arm around Dimitri's shoulders. "Did you need anything?"

Dimitri tilted his head to look at him. "I don't. I'm just wondering what's going on in that head of yours."

Haven hesitated. He wanted to talk this out, but he didn't think he could, not yet. Instead, he kissed Dimitri's forehead. "You should go to sleep."

"I'm not sleepy."

"You need rest to heal, though."

The smile Dimitri gave him was impish. "I'll sleep, but later. I'm fine, Haven. I promise." He hesitated, and Haven waited. "I just want to spend time with you. Is that so strange?"

Haven couldn't resist kissing him again. "It's not strange. I want to spend time with you, too."

"Then let's do it. It's not like we have anything else to do, right?"

Haven knew that they would have to leave this bedroom

eventually. They needed to talk to Thor, to have lunch, then dinner. Even though he wanted to keep Dimitri to himself, Dimitri deserved a lot more, and so did Haven. They deserved to find out if they could become friends with the other men in the apartment. They deserved to know if they could be together out of bed, too.

But for now, that was fine, and Haven pulled Dimitri closer to him, wrapping himself around him and kissing him. Dimitri's hands roamed, and Haven let him.

The rest of the world could wait. Right now, Haven wanted Dimitri, and Dimitri wanted him.

CHAPTER TWELVE

Dimitri felt good when he woke up the next morning. Hell, he felt perfect. He could even ignore the twinge of pain in his thigh as long as he continued waking up in Haven's arms.

They'd spent most of yesterday with the four men who were helping them, and Dimitri had started getting to know them. He now understood why Haven had called Thor. Even though they hadn't been friends, it was apparent even to Dimitri that Thor was a man of honor. He could easily have told Haven he couldn't help him, or that only Dimitri could come. Haven had expected that. Hell, he'd been planning on going back to the conclave.

Instead, Thor had convinced Haven to come with them, at least for now. He'd given Dimitri some respite and enough time to think about a way to change Haven's mind when it came to going back to the conclave. Cecil and Isaac were good men, too, and so was Tryg, even though he was a bit rougher than Thor. He was wary of Haven, and Dimitri understood why. He loved Isaac, and Isaac looked like he should be protected. Dimitri knew better than to assume that Isaac was weak. But from the way Tryg behaved with him, it was obvious that he considered himself his protector. He would make sure nothing happened to Isaac, and having Haven, a hero, with them, put him in danger. As far as Tryg was concerned, it put all of them in danger, and Dimitri was once again grateful he'd welcomed Haven anyway.

Dimitri didn't know what he would have done if he'd been

alone right now. It was easy to imagine what would have happened to Haven, though. He would have gone back to the conclave, and the conclave would have imprisoned him. If he was lucky, they would have put him on trial before killing him, but Dimitri wasn't sure about that. Haven seemed convinced of it, but would the conclave want other heroes to know about what was happening and possibly to realize Haven was right?

Dimitri had tangled with them often enough to know how they behaved. A few conclave members might have changed over time, but they were still the same self-serving, cruel assholes. They wouldn't care about Haven. The only thing they cared about was their power, and if word went out that one of their heroes had betrayed them because he'd thought they were doing the wrong thing, things could get dicey for them. They wouldn't want that to happen, and they would kill Haven before he could make people realize why he'd done it.

"Now it's you who's thinking too hard," Haven murmured. He pulled Dimitri closer to his chest and buried his face against the back of Dimitri's neck.

Dimitri closed his eyes and sighed in pleasure. He didn't know what he would do if he couldn't have this anymore. He'd only shared a bed with Haven twice, but it felt so right, and like he belonged. He didn't want to lose it.

He didn't want to lose Haven.

He wiggled until he could turn to face Haven. It was easy to ignore the slight pain in his thigh, and he focused on Haven, running a fingertip down Haven's nose, quickly kissing him and laughing at the way Haven wrinkled his nose. "What?" Dimitri asked.

"Morning breath."

Dimitri slapped a hand on his mouth. "I'm sorry. I didn't think." It was what Dimitri got for not being used to being with people.

"I meant me."

Dimitri chuckled and shook his head. "If you have morning breath, then I do, too."

"So maybe they cancel each other?" Haven pulled Dimitri even closer and kissed him, deeper this time. Dimitri hummed and opened his mouth to him, not caring one bit about morning breath. It wasn't pleasant, but it was worth it.

They kissed slowly because they had time. Dimitri couldn't remember the last time he'd been able to stay in bed until late without having to think about what was next. For now, he couldn't go back to work, and he wanted to take this time to enjoy life. It wouldn't last long. It never did. He also didn't know how much time he had with Haven, and he wanted to make the most of it.

When they separated, Dimitri was panting. He wanted more. He always wanted more with Haven, and he didn't know what to do with that. It made him feel like he wasn't steady on his feet, but also like maybe he didn't have to be. If he fell, Haven would catch him.

"Good morning," Haven murmured.

"Good morning." And it *would* be a good morning.

Haven rolled to his back and stretched, and Dimitri didn't even bother to act like he wasn't watching. Haven's body was perfect, and Dimitri's hands itched to get back on it.

He wasn't surprised Haven realized where his thoughts went, and he grinned at him, grabbing him and pulling him close again. "We should probably go to breakfast."

Dimitri smiled. "We could. Or we could stay in bed."

"And have Thor tease us?"

"I don't care if he teases us. Besides, the fact that he does means he cares. He's happy for you."

Haven wrinkled his nose again. "I don't understand it. He should send me back to the conclave. He should want me to die after what happened and everything I've done."

Dimitri wasn't ready for the conversation to take a serious turn, but he also wanted to address this. He cupped Haven's cheek, forcing him to look at him. "He knows what I know."

"And what's that?"

"That even though you made mistakes, it doesn't mean you're a bad man."

Haven snorted. "I wouldn't call killing people only because I was ordered to kill *mistakes*."

"But you regret it. There's nothing you can do to bring those people back to life, but you *can* work on the future and on making sure no one else gets hurt."

"I don't know if I can do that. I'm only one man, and the conclave is many."

"But you're not alone. You have me, and Thor, and Tryg, and even Cecil and Isaac."

Haven stared at Dimitri for a moment, and Dimitri waited. Haven needed time to wrap his mind around what he was saying.

"I have you, huh?" he eventually asked.

"You do. I'm not going anywhere." Not unless Haven wanted him to, and even then, he wasn't sure how he'd deal with that.

"I don't want you to go anywhere," Haven murmured. "I know what we're doing is crazy, but I feel like it's the right thing. Being with you feels right."

"Being with *you* feels right, too."

"I want to see where things will go. I want to see if we can work."

Dimitri couldn't help the wide smile that bloomed on his lips. "I want to see that too."

Haven pulled him closer, kissing him until Dimitri was panting.

"What about breakfast?" Dimitri asked between two kisses.

"It can wait. I'll take all the teasing in the world if it means I can have you."

Dimitri didn't protest. Why should he?

CHAPTER THIRTEEN

They stayed in the apartment only for a few days. It was soon evident to everyone that Dimitri wasn't doing well there, away from the forest, and Thor had been the one to suggest they move. Haven hadn't said no. How could he? He couldn't ignore Dimitri's well-being. That was the most important thing right now.

So they moved. Apparently, Thor and Tryg had a lot of houses and caves around the world, and that included a house deep in the forest. It was Thor's, as Tryg seemed to prefer caves, and it was big enough that the three couples each had their own bedroom.

A couple. Haven hadn't been part of a couple in a long time — since he was human, and he still wasn't sure how to deal with it. He wanted to make Dimitri happy all the time, but he was starting to wonder if he could. He hadn't been able to give Dimitri the forest, not the way Thor had. What else was Dimitri missing? What else wasn't he telling Haven?

Haven didn't know, and he didn't like that.

He also didn't know where Dimitri was, which was why he went to look for him. He wanted to check the wound, even though Dimitri had sworn he could do it by himself and that it was healing well. Haven trusted him, but he also wanted to make sure with his own two eyes that Dimitri wasn't trying to fool him.

He'd revealed too much, and Dimitri knew how guilty he felt. He suspected that if it helped him to not feel that way, Dimitri would hide a lot of things from him, and he didn't want that to happen. He didn't want to be in the dark. He had to know everything that was happening so he could make decisions based on facts rather than feelings.

Since the house was mostly empty, he headed outside. In the beginning, he'd been wary of letting Dimitri go out, even though that was why they were here. Thor had shown him how the security on the property worked, though. They would know if anyone came anywhere close to the house. There were cameras, and Cecil had used magic to ensure that no portals could be opened on the property. The conclave couldn't find them, at least not for now, and Haven had to relax. He and the others were here so that Dimitri could be in the forest, where he belonged. He couldn't forbid Dimitri to do just that.

He already knew Dimitri had a favorite spot, so he headed there. He heard the voices before he got to Dimitri, and he slowed his pace, wanting to make sure he didn't scare the three men. Isaac was especially skittish, even though he was obviously trying hard not to be, and the last thing Haven wanted was for Tryg to hate him even more than he already did.

"Can you do that again?" Isaac asked, his voice soft but stronger than Haven had ever heard it.

Dimitri laughed, and the sound made a shiver run down Haven's spine. He'd heard that laugh before, when they were in bed together, and he wanted to hear it over and over again.

"That's incredible," Cecil murmured, and Haven had to look at what was happening.

Isaac and Cecil were sitting on the ground, and a small rabbit was in front of them. Isaac was rubbing the top of the rabbit's head, and he squeaked when the rabbit shifted and became a wolf. He was wary for a second, then, the wolf—Dimitri—butted his head against Isaac's still raised hand, obviously asking for more cuddles.

Including today, Haven had seen Dimitri shift into three different animals. He was gorgeous in all of his forms, but seeing this now reminded Haven just how different they were.

He'd been able to avoid thinking about it when they were in bed together, even though Dimitri looked so different. Haven *knew* how different they were every time he saw the horns on Dimitri's head, every time he fell Dimitri's beard against his skin. He'd been able to push all of that to the back of his mind until now, though.

He couldn't anymore. He wasn't sure why. He'd already known Dimitri was a supernatural creature and that he could shift into different animals. Why did he feel so unsettled, then? He didn't know, but he didn't want to burden Dimitri or the other two men. He took a step back, heading away toward the house.

What he'd seen was a stark reminder that even though Dimitri wasn't a monster, he also wasn't a hero, and Haven shouldn't be with him. Haven wanted to, desperately, but they truly were different. Right now, they were both on the run, and it had pushed them together. It had created feelings they probably wouldn't be feeling otherwise.

Or would they?

Haven had a hard time believing those feelings were fake, but could they be real? He was a hero. It had been beaten and trained into him that he couldn't be in love and that he especially couldn't be in love with a supernatural creature. They were too different. Their worlds were miles apart, and even though they were trying, they couldn't fit together. There was no way for them to make it work.

No matter how much he wanted it to.

Haven rubbed his face. He shouldn't be thinking about this right now, but he knew that if he didn't, he would hurt Dimitri. If he wasn't planning on pursuing anything with Dimitri, he had to tell him now. He'd already been acting as if they were together and as if he would stay, and he understood how stupid it had been now. He'd promised Dimitri he would stick around for a bit, that he wouldn't confront the conclave, but he couldn't keep that promise. He truly wanted things to change. He wanted people like Dimitri to have a chance, even if they didn't save children. What they did didn't matter. It *shouldn't* matter. No, Dimitri didn't deserve to die, but it wasn't because he saved children. He didn't deserve to die because he hadn't done anything wrong. He didn't deserve to die only because he was a leshy rather than a human or a hero.

Haven couldn't give up. He had a chance—albeit a small one—to change things, to make the conclave see how wrong they were. Could he really not try? Could he keep running along with Dimitri?

He didn't know. He wanted to be sure, but he couldn't, and it was terrifying. He was a hero. That would never change, no matter how much he wished he could shed those responsibilities. He'd been a hero when he was born, and he would be a hero for the rest of his life. It didn't have anything to do with the work he did for the conclave. It was just who he was, just like Dimitri was a leshy.

Could they work together, or had Haven been fooling himself into thinking they could?

Dimitri shifted back to his human form. He couldn't stop smiling, and he didn't even try to.

Cecil grinned at him. "That's incredible."

"I'm sure you have incredible powers, too. I'm just me."

"And you can become a rabbit, a mouse, or a wolf," Isaac pointed out. "He's right. It *is* incredible." He pouted. "So I'm the only one who can't do anything."

Dimitri felt for him. Isaac was human, even though he was

immortal. He was the only human in their group, and it had to be strange. It wasn't a bad thing, though. "You don't have to be magical or to be able to shift to be special," he said.

Isaac wrinkled his nose. "I know. Tryg's already told me that. He loves me even though I'm human." His smile softened. "Some days, I think he loves me *because* I'm human. He's so used to supernatural things, but I'm not one of them, and he thinks he has to protect me from everything."

"Doesn't that get to be a bit too much sometimes?"

"No. I know it might be for some people, but I'm perfectly fine with it. I know I need to be protected. I don't know much about the supernatural world, and I'm not equipped to deal with it. Tryg is, though, and he'll always take care of me. I love him for it." He hesitated. "After everything that happened to me, I know I can stand on my own two feet, but I don't *have* to. I deserve to be loved. I deserve to be taken care of."

Cecil reached for Isaac, squeezing his hand. "You're right. You do deserve those things." Dimitri stayed out of the conversation. Isaac had briefly explained what had happened to him. He hadn't gone into details, but now Dimitri knew he'd been used as a sex slave for years. He could only imagine how awful that life had been, and he was happy that Isaac was out of it. He was also humbled that Isaac had opened up to him. That couldn't have been an easy thing to go through.

It made him realize that he wasn't alone anymore. He'd started this adventure, this thing he was doing with the children, alone. He was always alone, except for his animals. It was because of the children, but also because it was easier. The conclave wouldn't stop hunting him, and he'd never wanted to expose anyone to that. It wouldn't have been fair, especially since most of the people he knew were human. They weren't equipped to deal with the conclave.

Dimitri's new friends were, though.

Well, Isaac might not be, but Tryg would never allow anything to happen to him. He also wouldn't allow anything to happen to Dimitri, and neither would Thor, Haven, or even Isaac and Cecil.

Dimitri wasn't alone anymore. He had friends. He had a boyfriend. He had his entire life in front of him, and he couldn't wait. He was finally hopeful about something, and he still couldn't stop smiling as they headed back inside the house.

He would have to thank Thor once again for thinking about bringing them here. He'd been fine in the apartment, but in the middle of the forest, he felt *perfect*. It was his home, and for once, he wasn't alone in it. He didn't have to share it just with wolves. He could share it with people he considered friends.

When they stepped inside, they found Haven in the kitchen. Dimitri smiled at Isaac and Cecil, then made a beeline for him. He wrapped his arms around Haven, hugging him from the back, pressing his chest against him, but to his surprise, instead of teasing him or trying to kiss him, Haven tensed.

Something was wrong.

"What's going on?" Dimitri asked, stepping away.

Haven twisted on his stool. "Nothing. You had fun with Cecil and Isaac?"

Dimitri stared at Haven, trying to read him. He couldn't, not well. It was worrying, because Haven had finally stopped using the shield he usually had up against him in the past few days, and now, it was up again. Something had happened, but Dimitri didn't know what, and Haven wouldn't tell him. That much, Dimitri was sure of.

"Are you sure? Because you don't seem happy. Has something happened with the conclave?"

Haven shook his head and smiled at Dimitri, but Dimitri

could see it was forced. "I'm fine. I promise. Nothing happened. I'm worried, but I know they can't find us here. That doesn't mean I can forget about them, though. Don't mind me. It's ingrained in me to think about all the possibilities and the outcomes, and I don't like some of the ones I'm thinking about. That's all." He reached for Dimitri, and Dimitri allowed him to pull him into his arms. They hugged, wrapping around each other, and Dimitri closed his eyes and inhaled Haven's scent.

He wanted to believe Haven. He wanted to trust that he was only worried about the conclave and that nothing else was happening. It made sense, after all.

He couldn't help the glimmer of doubt that settled in his chest, though.

Was Haven already regretting what they were doing? Did he not want to be with Dimitri anymore?

Haven kissed the side of Dimitri's neck, and when Dimitri looked at him, he appeared more like the Haven he was getting used to. "You didn't answer me. Did you have fun outside?"

"I did." But Dimitri couldn't help but wonder what had happened while he'd been outside with Cecil and Isaac. Because something had, and Haven wasn't going to tell him, which meant it was bad.

CHAPTER FOURTEEN

Dimitri was spending time with Isaac and Cecil again. Haven was doing his best not to resent that, but he was failing, and he didn't like himself for it.

He understood why Dimitri spent more time with those two. Isaac might be human, but he was immortal, and he'd been with Tryg a while. Cecil was a supernatural creature, just like Dimitri. It was natural that Dimitri would want to spend time with him. From what Haven had understood, it had been a long time since he'd had the opportunity to spend time with someone like him. Dimitri didn't like talking about those things, though, so it was mostly a guess.

But Haven felt like they were running out of time. Eventually, he would have to stop hiding and face the conclave. He would have to leave Dimitri behind, and he doubted they would see each other again. He wanted to spend all the time he could with Dimitri, and that wasn't happening.

He wasn't about to tell Dimitri that, though.

Dimitri needed friends, and he finally had them. If Haven had done one good thing in this situation, it was that. He'd showed Dimitri that he could have more than what he had, that he could have people in his life, even with what he did. He had no doubt that Thor, Tryg, and the other two would help Dimitri with the children once Dimitri was healed, and they'd also help him stay away from the conclave. That was just the kind of men they were, and Haven knew they would take care of Dimitri when he wasn't there anymore.

Besides, the fact that Dimitri was spending more time with

Isaac and Cecil rather than with Haven was probably a sign that they didn't belong together. Haven had known that all along, and this was proof. He had to give Dimitri the space to spread his wings. He couldn't hold him back, not when he wouldn't be there for long. Dimitri belonged with people who were like him, who wielded supernatural powers, who didn't kill people just because of what they were. He should have better than Haven.

Haven didn't deserve him.

Haven had never thought he was a bad man, and he still didn't. He despised his past, though, and he would do anything to change it. Even though Dimitri didn't resent him for it, Haven did, and he didn't know if there was a way out of it. The only one he could see was talking to the conclave and trying to convince them that what they were doing was wrong. It wouldn't bring the people he'd killed back to life, but it would help their descendants and other supernatural creatures who were just trying to live their life.

He swallowed and looked at the closed bedroom door. He could have gone out there and spent time with Thor and Tryg, and they wouldn't have said anything. Well, Thor wouldn't have. Tryg wasn't exactly happy with Haven's presence in their little group, but he would have tolerated Haven. Instead, Haven was moping in the bedroom, and it had to stop.

Haven had to do something.

He already knew what he *should* do. Dimitri was finding his footing, and he wasn't alone anymore. That meant he would have support when Haven was gone, and the situation wouldn't get any better than how it already was.

It was time.

Haven wasn't about to call the conclave from inside the house, though, so he got to his feet. The forest was vast, and he no doubt could find a spot from which he could call. Of course, things weren't that easy because Thor saw him on his way out and stopped him.

"How are you holding up?" he asked.

Haven smiled. He couldn't do anything else. He had to make sure Thor didn't understand what he was doing. He didn't know why, but Thor didn't want him to go back to the conclave. He would try to stop him, just like he had before, but now Haven didn't have a reason to stick around. Dimitri was feeling better, and it was time for Haven to take up his responsibilities, for himself, but also for Dimitri, who deserved to live a life in which people wouldn't try to kill him.

"I'm fine," he said.

"You don't look fine. What is it? Have you and Dimitri fought?"

"We haven't."

"Then why do you look like someone killed your dog?" He paused. "Did someone *actually* kill your dog? Do you have a dog? Did you leave it with the conclave?"

Haven shook his head. Sometimes, he didn't know what to think of Thor. He was a lethal supernatural creature, yet he was also bouncy like a child. "I don't have a dog. Heroes can't have pets."

Thor wrinkled his nose. "There are so many rules you guys have to follow, and so many things you can't have. Do you even like being a hero?"

"It doesn't matter if I like it or not. It's my job. I'm a hero."

Thor waved Haven's words away. "I know, I know. You were born a hero, and you'll always be a hero. All of you guys think that way."

Haven wasn't surprised Thor knew about it. "Exactly. I can't change what I am."

"You can't change what you are, but you can change the way you behave. The fact that you were born a hero doesn't mean you have to be static. It's like me being a draugr. I can choose to be whoever I want to be, even though I can't change *what* I am."

Thor didn't understand. People seldom did. Heroes weren't just another kind of supernatural creature. They were born to defend humanity. It was the only reason they came into the world, and if Haven wasn't one, he didn't know *what* he was. Probably nothing. "Did you need something?" he asked.

Thor stared at him for a moment, then shook his head. "I didn't. I was just checking in on you."

Haven was touched. He didn't understand why these people cared about him as much as they did, but he wasn't going to complain. It didn't make sense, but it meant they would be there for Dimitri when he wasn't anymore. "I'm going for a walk."

"Should I tell Dimitri that when he comes looking for you?"

"You can, but I doubt he will."

Thor frowned. "Why? Are you jealous that he's spending time with Cecil? Because you have no reason to be."

"Of course not. He deserves to have friends. He hasn't had an easy life."

Thor nodded. "I can't promise the rest of his life will be easy, but he won't be alone anymore. I hope you know that."

"I do." Maybe Thor suspected what Haven was doing. Either way, he didn't try to stop Haven as he stepped outside. Haven took a deep breath, then looked around, trying to find a spot in which he would have some privacy. Once he had, he took out his phone.

It was strange. He hadn't contacted the conclave in a while, and he felt like he shouldn't, yet also that he should. He had to explain what was going on. He didn't have a way out of it, and he was done running. He was a hero, and he should act like one.

Dimitri knew something was wrong, but he had no idea what, or what to do about it. He wanted to fix things with Haven. He had to. What happened next in his life would include Haven, too, even though it probably shouldn't.

Dimitri had allowed himself to fall in love with Haven, and now, there was no getting out of it. He couldn't forget his feelings. He couldn't forget *Haven*, even if he had left him behind.

He had no intention of doing that.

He and Haven were together. They were a unit, and they had to face whatever was next together. Dimitri couldn't deny Haven had retreated, though. He still had no idea what had happened, why Haven was behaving this way, but he knew the only way to find out was to ask. Haven might not answer, but he also might, and Dimitri had to know. He couldn't fix it otherwise.

"What's going on with you? Is your thigh hurting?" Isaac asked.

Dimitri forced himself to smile. "My thigh's fine. Thanks."

Isaac frowned. "There *is* a problem, though."

Dimitri hesitated. He didn't usually talk to people about his problems, but that was mostly because he never had anyone to talk them through with. He wasn't sure Haven would like Dimitri talking about him to Cecil and Isaac, but Dimitri wanted to. He wanted to know what they thought about the situation, if they believe it could work, and he trusted them to keep anything he told them to themselves.

He swallowed. "I'm not sure what's going on," he eventually explained. "I just know that something *is* happening with Haven, and I don't know what to do about it."

Isaac's expression shifted into comprehension. "He became distant."

Dimitri blinked. "You noticed?"

Isaac's smile held a bit of pity, and Dimitri didn't like it. "I think we all noticed how he was behaving. Do you know what happened?"

"I have no idea."

"Did you ask him?" Cecil asked.

Dimitri nodded. "I tried, but he hasn't answered. He brushes me off every time, telling me everything is fine."

"But everything isn't fine." Cecil leaned back against the couch.

They were in the living room upstairs, because it was quieter and the room was smaller. There was a big living room downstairs in which they spent time together with everyone else, but during the day, when it was just the three of them, this was perfect. Dimitri felt more at home and protected in this room, which was what he needed right now.

Isaac leaned toward Dimitri and patted his hand. "You should talk to him. It's the only way you'll know what he's thinking, and the same goes for him. Neither of you can read minds. You have to talk this out if you want things to work between the two of you."

He was right. "It's been so long since I've had a relationship. Most days, I feel like I don't know what I'm doing."

Isaac's smile was wistful. "I'd never had a relationship before Tryg. I'm still learning, but I do know that communication is key. If you want to know what's going on with Haven, you're going to have to push until he tells you. It can be hard, but it needs to be done."

Dimitri was going to try, but he doubted Haven would allow him to break through. Whatever had happened to him, it had made him put up his shield again, and everyone was left out, including Dimitri. He was pulling away from all of them, and that could only mean one thing—he was getting ready to leave.

Dimitri hoped that wasn't the case. He couldn't deal with that, not right now, not since it would mean Haven's death.

But Isaac was right. If he wanted to find out what was happening, if he wanted to find a way out of the rut that he and Haven were in, he would have to talk to Haven. They would need to be honest with each other, and hopefully, it would be enough to fix things and to keep Haven here.

Dimitri wasn't sure it would be, though. He also wasn't sure what he would do if Haven decided to leave anyway.

He was going to find out. He had to. He had to do this and to be there for Haven, whatever Haven decided. He might not share Haven's belief that the conclave would listen to him, but he couldn't ignore that part of Haven's life. The only thing he could do was support him and protect him as much as he could, and that was what he would try to do.

He didn't know if he would succeed.

Haven couldn't remember the last time he'd been so frightened. Maybe when he and Dimitri had been on the run, before contacting Thor. He'd been scared for Dimitri that time, though, while now, he was scared for himself.

He had no way to know how Marsha would react to his phone call. He didn't think she could trace it, but still. What he was about to do would make or break the rest of his life. It might give him a chance to talk to the conclave and convince them that not all supernatural creatures were evil, but it also might lead to his death. It might lead to him having to live without Dimitri.

Because he had no doubt that even if the conclave agreed to listen to him and give him a chance to explain, they wouldn't allow him to be with Dimitri. They might be ready to admit that not all supernatural creatures should die, but from that to having a hero be in a relationship with one was a step they would never take. It meant Haven was going to have to choose.

He didn't know if he could.

Now wasn't the time to make that decision, though. Now was the time to focus on what he was doing, and he quickly dialed Marsha's number before he could think better of it and change his mind.

It rang a few times, surprisingly. Marsha always answered right away, or as soon as she could. This time, though, she wasn't, and it made Haven worry.

"Haven," Marsha said.

He took a second to breathe in and out, then said, "Marsha. I was hoping to talk to you."

"I bet you were. What's going on, Haven? Mather came back from his mission telling me that you attacked him."

"I did."

"Yet instead of being on the run, you're calling me. What's going on?"

"I already told you what was going on. Dimitri doesn't deserve to die. He's doing our job. He's protecting children, and I don't want him to get hurt and have to stop."

"And you had to wound one of your fellow heroes to make that happen?"

"I had to, since the conclave sent him before I was even done with the mission."

"You can't say they were wrong, though. They didn't trust you to do your job, and you didn't do it." She sighed, and for the first time ever, Haven could hear the weariness in her voice. "I don't know what you want from me, Haven. I realize Dimitri doesn't deserve to die. I also realize the conclave won't just take my word for it, though. How would I know? I haven't met him."

Haven blinked. He hadn't expected this, but it made him hope. "I could talk to them. I could explain what Dimitri does, why he does it. They have to know that not all supernatural creatures are evil, no matter what we've been thinking."

"And you think you'll be able to convince them of that?"

"I'm going to try. It's the only thing I can do. Dimitri is trying to do a good thing. He shouldn't pay for that. Heroes are supposed to protect humanity, and we're not doing a good job, not if a supernatural creature has to step in and do it for us."

There was a pause, and Haven wondered if he'd pushed too hard. He was relieved when Marsha said, "You're right. Your job is to protect humanity. You should come back and talk to the conclave. I can't promise they'll listen to you, but I'm sure we can work things out. You shouldn't throw away all the work you've done. You've been a hero for hundreds of years. You've saved people during that time. You can continue doing so."

"I can't continue killing supernatural creatures, though. Not if they don't deserve it."

"I'm sure we can find a way around it. It won't be possible if you're on the run, though. The conclave already doesn't trust you. You have to take the next step and show them they can."

"And the only way for me to do that is to come back?"

"I think so."

It could be a trap. Haven wasn't stupid. He wanted to believe that Marsha and the conclave would welcome him back with open arms, but how could he? They'd sent Mather to kill him and Dimitri. He wouldn't have hesitated, either, if he and Haven hadn't somewhat been friends. But his presence told Haven everything he needed to know about the conclave.

Not about Marsha, though. He'd worked for her for decades, and she'd never let him down. Of course, he had never let her down, either, not until now. He'd run away. He'd disobeyed orders. He'd wounded another hero, and then he'd run away again. He was protecting a supernatural creature who was supposed to die per conclave orders.

He didn't know if there was anything he could do in this situation. He was willing to try, though. He had to choose between Dimitri and the conclave, and right now, he wasn't sure that staying with Dimitri was the best thing he could do.

He was in love with a leshy. He couldn't deny that, not anymore, not to himself. He was in love with *Dimitri*, and that meant he had to leave him. They couldn't be together. They were too different, and Haven was a hero. His entire life was built around that fact. He didn't have a life if he wasn't a hero anymore, and he wouldn't know what to do with himself.

This was his chance to go back to his old life. He would have to leave Dimitri behind, but Dimitri wasn't alone anymore. He would have his friends, and he would forget Haven soon. He would have to. Haven was sure there was someone more suited to be with Dimitri out there in the world, and Dimitri would find them and be happy.

Haven swallowed. The thought of Dimitri with someone else made his mouth taste bitter, and it almost pushed him to tell Marsha he was never coming back.

For the first time ever, he didn't *want* to go back. He wanted to forget about his responsibilities, about his past, about what he would abandon if he left the conclave and the heroes behind. He wanted to be selfish and to think only about his happiness.

He couldn't. He wasn't alone in this relationship, but there was more to it, too. If Haven decided he didn't want to be a hero anymore, it would put humanity at risk. He was only one hero, of course, but he still did good work.

He *had* to go back, no matter how little he wanted it or how risky it was. It was his destiny, and while he'd been happy with Dimitri for a few weeks, he'd always known it couldn't last. Better to leave now that they were okay with each other and that Dimitri was safe than wait for them to start fighting and hate each other.

He cleared his throat. Even though he'd made his decision, the words were hard to push out. "I'll come back," he told Marsha.

Dimitri had only heard the end of the conversation, but he didn't have to ask to know what was happening. He waited until Haven hung up to confront him, though. He'd wanted to throw himself at him as soon as he heard the words, but he couldn't.

He shouldn't have trusted Haven, not with his heart. He only had himself to blame. Haven had been honest with him. He'd told him that eventually, he would go back to the conclave, and from the sound of it, it was a good thing, at least for Haven. Dimitri wasn't sure how, but the conclave seemed to have realized they should welcome Haven back into their ranks, and of course Haven wasn't going to say no. He was a hero. That was his entire life while being with Dimitri had only been a pleasant interlude. Dimitri should have known better than to expect anything else.

He hadn't.

He shook his head. "You called the conclave," he said, stepping from between the trees.

Haven jerked, a sign that he hadn't been careful with his surroundings. He'd been entirely focused on the phone call, and that made Dimitri feel even worse.

Haven had always told him he was planning on going back. He was a hero, and he felt that he belonged with the conclave, doing his job. Dimitri shouldn't blame Haven for falling in love with him. He'd allowed himself to do that, and Haven didn't have anything to do with it.

Haven put away his phone. "I called my superior."

"What did she say?"

"She told me to come back. The conclave isn't happy, but

she thinks we can work things out."

"She doesn't think they'll kill you?" Dimitri had a hard time believing that, but he wanted to hope that was the case. Not for himself—never for himself because it meant he was losing the man he'd fallen in love with—but for Haven. He was the only man Dimitri felt comfortable with, a man with whom he could have shared his life. Instead, he was losing him, and there was nothing he could do.

He truly should have known better.

Haven shrugged. "She didn't say it would be easy, but yeah. She thinks there's a chance."

"What if she's wrong?"

"I know you think the conclave won't listen to me because they didn't listen to you, but you're a supernatural creature. I'm a hero. It's different."

That shouldn't have hurt as much as it did. Dimitri knew Haven was right. The conclave hadn't listened to him, but that might only be because he was a supernatural creature and they were convinced he was trying to trick them. Of course, if Haven wanted to convince them not to kill supernatural creatures on sight, it might have been a good idea for the conclave to actually listen to one, but what did Dimitri know? He wasn't a hero. He was just a leshy.

"I think I can do good," Haven said, stepping closer and reaching for Dimitri.

Dimitri took a step back. There was a flash of pain on Haven's face, but he quickly hid it. Dimitri didn't like that he was hurting Haven, but it was either that or hurt himself by allowing Haven to come even closer.

He couldn't do that.

"It won't be easy. I'm not saying it will be. I want to do everything I can to change the way things work, though," Haven continued. "I promise I'll be back."

Dimitri shook his head. "We both know that's an empty

promise. Once you're with the conclave again, you'll go back to your life, your job, and you'll forget about me."

"How could I forget about you?"

"The same way I'll forget about you. We both knew we weren't meant to be together from the beginning. It was nice while it lasted." Dimitri was surprised Haven couldn't hear the sound of his heart breaking. He felt like it showed in every word he said, in his expression, in every molecule in his body.

Maybe that was why Haven stepped closer to him again and reached for his hand.

Dimitri couldn't allow it to happen. He was losing Haven, and it was obvious that nothing he could say would change Haven's mind. He had to be strong. He had to stand tall and make Haven see that he could go on even without him.

Besides, being in love with Haven didn't make sense. They'd only been together a few weeks. They had been weeks of bliss as far as Dimitri was concerned, but obviously, they hadn't meant the same for Haven. That was okay. Dimitri should have known better than to allow himself to fall in love. He should have known better than to open himself up to this kind of pain.

"This doesn't mean we can't be together," Haven murmured. "I still want to be with you. I don't think that's ever going to change."

"It's going to have to. The conclave won't allow you to be with me. Even if by some miracle they listen to you and agree they shouldn't kill supernatural creatures just because of what they are, there's no way they'll allow a hero to be with one."

Haven's expression told Dimitri he was aware of that.

Dimitri shook his head again, then moved away. "Don't bother coming back. You made your choice."

"Why can't I have both? I'll never stop being a hero, but it doesn't mean I can't be with you. If I managed to convince the conclave, I'm sure they won't care."

"That's not true. The choice was either to be with me and be free or to go back to the conclave and never see me again. You knew that."

Haven crossed his arms over his chest. "You never told me it was a choice. You knew I wanted to go back."

"I also thought you would be smarter than to throw yourself back into their hands. I thought you knew it was a choice between me or the conclave, and you've obviously made it." Dimitri paused, hope tightening his chest. "Unless you're going to change your mind now that you know you *have* a choice?"

Haven shook his head. "I have to do this. I have to try. It's the only way for me to atone for what I did in the past."

"But don't you see? You don't have to atone. You don't have anything to atone *for*. This is only going to end with you dying, and I can't deal with that. Do you really think the conclave will welcome you back? They can't. You went against their orders. You went against everything they've worked toward for hundreds of years, possibly longer. How can they welcome you back? They won't listen to you, Haven. They can't, not if they want to keep their power, and that's the only reason they were created. You think heroes should protect humanity, and you might not be wrong, but the conclave is an entirely different thing."

Haven no doubt knew the history of the conclave better than Dimitri, but it wouldn't change anything. He'd made his choice, and he'd chosen the conclave. Not Dimitri.

Never him.

Haven looked heartbroken, but he didn't protest, not again. "I'll miss you," he murmured.

Dimitri looked away and pressed his lips together. He was going to miss Haven like he would miss a limb—or his heart. He couldn't say those words to Haven, though. It was already hard enough as it was. It was hard both for him and for Haven, and he didn't want to make things even worse.

But no matter what Haven thought or was trying to convince himself of, Dimitri was losing him. There was no chance for them to see each other again, ever. The conclave would kill Haven, and then, Dimitri would be left alone.

He had to do something. He couldn't give up.

But when he turned around, Haven was already gone.

Haven ran away. He wasn't proud of it, but he couldn't see a way around it. He couldn't stay with Dimitri, not after their conversation, and not when Marsha was waiting for him.

He'd always known he would have to choose. Whatever he'd told Dimitri, he knew that if he went back to the conclave, he couldn't stay with Dimitri. It hadn't been a problem in the beginning, when Haven hadn't cared for Dimitri—when he hadn't loved him—but it was now. Haven's heart was breaking.

Yet he wasn't planning on going back.

He couldn't. He could make a difference. He hoped that with Marsha's support, the conclave would allow him to speak, that they would listen to him and finally understand. Haven had killed so many supernatural creatures, and while some of them had deserved it, most hadn't. He'd been following orders that shouldn't have been given, orders he should have questioned. If he had, he wouldn't have killed so many innocent souls. Instead, he'd done as he was told, and he was a murderer. If there was even one chance that he could fix this, make things better, he wanted to do it.

Even if it broke his heart.

He might always have known he would have to leave Dimitri behind, but he'd hoped against all odds. Dimitri was right, though. Even if the conclave did listen to Haven, they wouldn't allow him to be with Dimitri. They couldn't, not when heroes weren't allowed to have relationships. They could have sex, but that was where things ended, and most of them didn't even bother. Meaningless sex didn't help. It wasn't a relationship. It didn't keep them warm at night, give them what they needed.

And now, Haven had lost Dimitri. He'd had him for a bit, and he was alone again.

But he was a hero, and he'd always been alone. He could deal with it. He would have to.

He was relieved when no one was in the house when he went back inside. He hurried to the bedroom he shared with Dimitri, packing the few things he'd accumulated over the weeks. There wasn't much, and before Dimitri could come back, Haven was out of the house again. This time, he headed toward the edge of the property, knowing he wouldn't be able to open a portal unless he stepped off it. He did so as soon as he reached its edge, and then he was gone.

He opened a portal into the forest in which he'd first met Dimitri, one the conclave wouldn't be able to trace. He might be going back, but that didn't mean he wanted the conclave to know where Dimitri was.

He stepped through the portal, then stared at it, knowing it was the last thing that tied him to Dimitri.

He closed it.

His heart shattered when the portal disappeared. He wasn't an idiot, and he knew Dimitri and the others would leave the house as soon as they could. They couldn't trust that Haven wouldn't tell the conclave where they were, and that meant that Haven wouldn't be able to go back. He'd lost Dimitri, and it was his own fault.

He swallowed and opened a second portal, this time, one the conclave would know about.

Then he stepped through.

He appeared in the middle of the conclave building in which he'd lived before. Everyone seemed to stop moving around him, but he ignored them, walking toward Marsha's office. He didn't make it there. Two heroes stepped in front of him, and he waited, knowing Marsha would come. He wasn't surprised the heroes didn't trust him, and for once, he didn't care. He wasn't here to continue doing what he'd done before. He was here to talk to the conclave, to convince them to stop what they were doing. Even if it meant he was never trusted again, it didn't matter. He would have done what he had to do.

"Haven," Marsha said as she strode toward him.

"I came back, just like I told you I would."

She nodded, and to Haven's surprise, she was smiling. "I knew I could count on you. I already sent a team to the place in which you opened the portal. I have to say I didn't expect the leshy to still stay around there, but I'm glad you convinced him to. Capturing him will be the sign the conclave needs to know they can trust you and welcome you back in our ranks."

Haven took a step back, dread making his stomach feel like lead. "You sent a team into the forest?"

Marsha's gaze went hard. "We have to catch that leshy. And like I said, if you want the conclave to welcome you back, this is the price you have to pay."

"It's not why I came back. I came back to talk to the conclave, to make them see that Dimitri and most other supernatural creatures aren't dangerous. We don't have a reason to kill them."

Someone sucked in a breath, but Haven kept his gaze on Marsha.

"You allowed the leshy to influence you. I thought you'd come to your senses, but clearly, I was wrong."

Haven shook his head. "I told you that was why I wanted

to come back. I explained to you the situation with Dimitri. I thought you understood." But she hadn't. No one would understand, not anyone who was standing there watching Haven. He should have known better. He should have trusted Dimitri, but he'd thought he could change things.

Instead, he might have condemned Dimitri—and himself.

At least he'd used two different portals. There was no way the conclave would be able to trace the first one, but Haven couldn't stay here. They'd showed their true colors, and so had Marsha, someone Haven had trusted with his own life more than once.

He shook his head and stepped back, throwing his hand to the side to open another portal. "I thought I could trust you," he told Marsha.

"I thought I could trust you, too. But since it's obvious I can't, you will have to be stopped." Before Haven could do anything, someone grabbed his arm. He tried to open the portal anyway, but then the heroes were on him, pushing him to the ground, handcuffing his hands behind his back. He tried to fight, to go back to Dimitri, to warn him of what was happening, but he couldn't.

He was a prisoner. He was imprisoned by the same people he'd trusted for so many years, by people he'd thought respected him enough to listen to him. He'd fought next to most of the heroes hauling him up and pushing him against the wall, and this was how they behaved. He'd trusted them, and now, he saw he'd been wrong.

Marsha stepped closer. "I'm sorry it had to come to this. I thought you understood, but clearly, I was wrong." She looked behind Haven. "Take him to one of the cells. I'll let the conclave know he's here."

There was nothing Haven could do but allow himself to be dragged away. He knew that no matter how much he fought, he couldn't break the handcuffs or the hold the two heroes had on him.

They wouldn't change their minds even if he explained. The conclave was too deep inside them. They had taken over a long time ago, and Haven had been a fool for thinking he could make them see the truth.

CHAPTER FIFTEEN

It was the first time Haven had been on this side of the cells. He'd locked up numerous supernatural creatures, even a few heroes, but he'd never thought he would be in their place. Now he could only watch as the heroes in the hallway on the other side of his cell door talked to each other, their voices soft, but not soft enough that he couldn't hear what they were saying.

They were talking about him.

He almost snorted, but he didn't want to get their attention. By now, the entire building had to be abuzz about what he'd done. Haven hadn't exactly been the golden child of heroes, but he'd been close. He'd been here for a long time, and while he'd been wounded more than once, he was still standing, and he still had all his limbs. He'd never been one to disobey orders, not until Thor, and now he'd done it again, and spectacularly.

He still didn't regret it. He didn't want to die, but if he died for the right reason, then he could make his peace with it. Of course, if he could choose, he would go back to Dimitri and spend the rest of his life with him—a very long life, since both of them were immortal. But it didn't look like he'd have a chance to do that, and he would have to deal with it. At least he wouldn't have to be alone for too long. He doubted the conclave would wait before they put him on trial and eventually executed him.

Dimitri had been right. The conclave wouldn't listen. Haven still hoped to be able to say his piece at the trial, but right now, he wasn't sure about anything anymore. Marsha had promised him everything would be okay, and he'd believed her. He'd trusted her, and she'd thanked him by sending a team to get Dimitri behind his back. She wouldn't be happy when she realized Haven had played her and that Dimitri wasn't in the forest in which Haven had opened the portal to come back. The conclave would be angry, too, and Haven suspected they would demand he tell them where Dimitri was.

He had no idea.

From what he knew about Thor and Tryg, they wouldn't have hesitated to relocate as soon as they realized Haven was gone. It would have been the right thing to do, which meant that the house in which Haven and Dimitri had been so happy was now empty. Even if somehow the conclave managed to get information out of Haven, they wouldn't get to Dimitri.

Dimitri was never far from Haven's thoughts. Haven was terrified that something had happened to him, even though he knew that probably wasn't the case. But what if the conclave had been too fast? What if they'd somehow found Dimitri and the others, had captured them, or worse, killed them?

The conclave wanted Dimitri dead, even though it didn't make sense. Haven wanted to hope Dimitri was alive, but he knew that when the conclave wanted something, they usually got it, and that meant Dimitri, too, eventually.

Haven was surprised they hadn't gotten him already.

He didn't understand, and he didn't care. The reason why they wanted to catch Dimitri so badly wasn't important. What *was* important was that Dimitri was hopefully safe and far away.

This was all Haven's fault. Because of him, Dimitri was on the run again. He hadn't listened, either to Dimitri or Thor or to himself.

Because Haven had known—no matter how much he'd

hoped, he'd known the conclave wouldn't be easy to deal with. He wasn't surprised they'd imprisoned him, even though he'd hoped for a different outcome.

And now he would probably die, and if anything happened to Dimitri, he would have caused his death, too. Possibly the death of Thor, Cecil, Tryg, and Isaac, too, and that wasn't something Haven could live with. If he caused the death of the five people who treated him like a person instead of a weapon, who had welcomed him into their lives, who had made him see there could be more to it than the conclave and killing, he would never forgive himself.

But he wouldn't have to live with the guilt for long. There was no doubt the conclave would execute him eventually, and since they wanted to make sure that no other hero got weird ideas about them and their orders, they would do it as soon as possible.

Haven sighed and went to sit on the hard bench in the corner. There was nothing else he could do. He had to wait to talk to the conclave. It wouldn't do him any good to try talking to the heroes who were still staring at him. He'd fought with one of them several times, but he could tell that anything he said would fall on deaf ears. Edana didn't want to listen to him. She and the other heroes thought he was corrupted — that Dimitri had somehow got to him and changed him. They thought he wasn't a hero anymore, and maybe they weren't wrong. As it was, though, Haven didn't care. Being a bad hero meant he didn't kill innocent supernatural creatures anymore, and he was ready to be just that. He couldn't stop being a hero, but he *could* stop hurting people.

He sat on the bench and leaned his head against the wall. He closed his eyes, wondering what next. How long would the conclave make him wait here? Would they let him know if they caught Dimitri? He'd been careful not to show Marsha how much he cared for Dimitri, but he might have failed. She had to wonder why he'd changed so much for one of the supernatural creatures he was supposed to kill. It could be only because of the children, but Marsha was smart. She would poke and prod until she got answers and the truth out of Haven, or out of Dimitri if she somehow managed to get to him.

Haven had made a mess of things. Only a few hours ago, he'd woken up with Dimitri wrapped around him. They'd made love, and he'd had his entire life in front of him. A life with Dimitri, with friends, doing the right thing rather than the easy one. Now he'd ruined everything. He'd lost his chance at love and happiness.

The sound of heels clicking on the floor made him sit up. He opened his eyes, waiting, and he wasn't surprised when Marsha appeared on the other side of the cell door.

He didn't bother getting to his feet. He normally would have, but she'd lost the respect he had for her when she betrayed him.

She arched a brow but didn't comment on his lack of respect. "Haven. Did you come to your senses?"

"I should be asking the same of you. I thought you trusted me, that you believed me when I told you Dimitri didn't deserve to die."

Marsha's eyes narrowed. "So now you're calling the leshy by his name? You two got closer than I expected."

Haven almost got to his feet. He was angry, but he didn't want Marsha to see how important Dimitri was to him. He didn't want her or the conclave to use Dimitri as leverage if they managed to get to him. "I call him Dimitri because he's a friend. He showed me what he does, Marsha. He showed me the children he saved, the bruises, the cigarette burns, the abuse. He might have gone about this the wrong way by killing the parents, but I can't say I'm sorry about that, either. You might not know much about humanity anymore, since you've been a hero for far longer than me and you seem to have left your feelings behind, along with your humanity, but those abusers would eventually get their hands back on their children, and they would continue hurting them. As far as I'm concerned, Dimitri is way too gentle with them."

"Too gentle? He tears them apart."

"His wolves do, and they do it because they know it's best for everyone, especially the children."

Marsha shook her head, looking halfway between perplexed and disgusted. "Enough of this. The conclave wants to talk to you tomorrow, so prepare yourself."

Haven sucked in a breath. That was sooner than he'd expected, yet not, and he didn't know if it was a good or a bad thing.

"They were in the forest where you and Haven met."

Dimitri stared at Thor, not knowing what to say, or even if he could say anything at all. "What do you mean?" he finally asked.

"Just what I said. Since I suspected something would happen, but also that Haven would never lead the conclave to us, I monitored the forest in which the two of you met. There was some activity there. Several portals opened, and heroes came through. Of course, they had to leave empty-handed, but that's enough for us to know that something *has* happened."

"Maybe Haven told them about it." Dimitri didn't want to believe that, but what did he know? Haven had run. He'd run away from him, from what they had. Maybe he'd been the one to tell the conclave where to find him. Haven was a hero after all, and he'd gone home. He'd known things wouldn't be good for him, yet he'd still gone, maybe because he was stupidly noble, or because it had been his plan all along.

No. Dimitri couldn't think that way. Even though Haven had been stupid, he'd been doing what he thought was right.

He would never have told the conclave where Dimitri and the others were. That just wasn't him, and Dimitri had to believe it. He had to believe the Haven he knew was the real Haven.

Otherwise, he would go nuts.

Thor reached over the table and awkwardly patted Dimitri's arm. "I don't think he told the conclave where we are. They haven't found the house yet, and I'm monitoring that, too. To me, it looks like he opened two portals — one the conclave couldn't detect, and another they could. That way, they thought he came in from the forest in which you met."

"So they have no idea about us?"

"I think so. Of course, we're still going to be cautious, but I doubt Haven would give you up to the conclave, no matter what they promise."

Dimitri sighed. He wanted to believe that, but he didn't know what to think anymore. He believed he and Haven had something, something important, something that would lead them to have a future together if Haven ever came back. He'd told Dimitri he wants to atone for what he'd done over the years, and while Dimitri didn't believe he had to, he understood where Haven came from. Still, Haven was gone, and he was out of Dimitri's reach.

"How are you feeling?" Isaac asked.

Dimitri laughed, but it wasn't a happy sound. "I have no idea how I'm feeling. Okay, at least physically." His thigh burned a bit, but it was nothing next to the pain in his heart.

"I'm sorry he left you."

"I always knew he would leave me. We weren't meant to be together."

Isaac, bless his heart, frowned. "Why not? Is it because you're a supernatural creature?"

"Exactly. Heroes are created to kill us. What we had was a small miracle, and I never expected it to last."

"You wanted it to, though."

Dimitri couldn't lie, so he didn't say anything.

"I'm sure that once he finds out the conclave tried to grab you, he'll come back. He'll know they're no good, not even for him," Cecil commented.

"He always knew they were no good. He knew they probably wouldn't listen to him, yet he went back anyway," Dimitri pointed out. "I don't think it'll change anything."

"You can't know that. He might not care about his own safety, but he cares about yours. He won't be happy that the conclave sent someone to catch you."

"It still doesn't mean he'll have the opportunity to do anything." Because Dimitri doubted the conclave had welcomed Haven back. And if they hadn't, it meant he was probably in jail, awaiting trial, or worse, already dead.

Dimitri sucked in a breath. He couldn't think that way. He had to keep his hopes up, even though it was the hardest thing he'd ever done.

Haven wasn't coming back. That much, Dimitri was sure of. And even if Haven wanted to come back, he wouldn't know where they were once they moved, and the conclave would never allow him to set foot outside the conclave building again.

Not alive, anyway.

Dimitri had to distract himself, so he was thankful when Thor's phone rang. Thor took it out of his pocket, frowned even harder than he already had been, and answered. "What?" he asked.

Dimitri couldn't hear the other side of the conversation, but he could guess from Thor's expression that it wasn't good.

"All right. Keep an eye out for me, will you? And please, stay safe. I don't want to lose you." There was a pause, then Thor laughed. "Yes, even though you're a hero. Take care," he added before hanging up.

Everyone's attention was on him. "Who was that?" Tryg

asked. "You sounded very friendly with them."

"It was my contact in the heroes."

There was a moment of silence, then Tryg asked, "You have a contact within the heroes? How many of them have you gathered over the years?"

"That doesn't matter. I've always had someone in the heroes because I knew I needed someone there. I had to know what the conclave was doing and what they were planning."

He turned to Dimitri. "And now, I know. They jailed Haven."

Dimitri swallowed once, then again. He wanted to speak, but he suspected his voice would be more a croak than anything. "They jailed him?"

"That's what my contact said, yes. But from what she heard, he's already being brought in front of the conclave. That means that one way or another, things will end soon."

Dimitri got up from his chair. "You mean they're going to kill him soon. Because we both know that's what they're going to do. There's no way they'll listen to him, not when it comes to this. They'll come up with an excuse, tell everyone that I corrupted him, something like that. Then no one will listen to him, and they'll get rid of him quietly so that he doesn't inspire other heroes." He stopped pacing and looked at the others gathered around the table. "I have to go. I have to do something to help him. I can't let him die, not for me. He was trying to do the right thing, and I won't abandon him."

Even if Dimitri had to do this on his own, it wouldn't stop him. Only death would at this point, and he thought there was a good chance that would happen this time, especially if he went into the conclave building. But for Haven, he was ready to do it. He was ready to sacrifice his life and much more to save the man he loved.

Chapter Sixteen

Haven was seeing the conclave today.

An envoy had talked to him yesterday. He'd asked why Haven had done what he'd done and whether he regretted it. Haven had explained, so the conclave knew what had happened, and they no doubt already formed an opinion. The trial wouldn't be a long one.

Haven was ready for anything they would dump on him, even death.

He'd barely slept. He would have preferred to sleep, because that way, he wouldn't have had to think about Dimitri the entire time. But on the other hand, he might have dreamed of him, and he wasn't sure how he'd have dealt with that.

His last memories of Dimitri weren't good ones. They'd fought, and Dimitri had tried to stop Haven from leaving. He'd tried to save Haven's life, and he'd failed because Haven was an idiot. He could have had a wonderful life with Dimitri and their friends, but instead, his life would be cut short.

Or would it? He'd lived a long time — hundreds of years — and while he hadn't done much good in his life, he'd still tried, especially recently. He wouldn't be dying prematurely. If anything, he'd be hundreds of years late.

He still felt like he hadn't even started living.

When the conclave had found him when he was still human, he'd thought that becoming a hero was the only thing he could do. It had brought his family money, and they'd been able to live comfortably while he went to train. He'd known he would never see them again, and he hadn't. He'd also known he'd done the right thing, though. With the money his parents had been given, they'd been able to raise Haven's siblings without too many problems. They hadn't gone hungry. They'd had a roof over their heads.

And Haven had become a professional killer.

Because that was what he was, what he'd been for so many years. The conclave might not like what Thor and Tryg did, but they weren't any different. They killed. And to do that, they used heroes. They told the heroes who they wanted dead, and the heroes obeyed without asking questions. In Haven's eyes, that made them equal to Thor and Tryg, yet worse because of who they killed.

At least Thor only chose people who deserved to die. Haven had talked to both him and Tryg enough times to know they only went after people who hurt other people, who didn't care about humanity. Haven, on the other hand, had killed supernatural creatures who hadn't done anything to deserve it. They'd all been trying to live their life as well as they could in the human world, and Haven had broken their dreams. He'd destroyed families, lives, things that could have been. He'd done it all because he trusted the conclave and believed they knew what they were doing.

It was an excuse, though. He should have questioned them. He should have asked why he was doing what he was doing. It would have meant he would die sooner, but would that have been such a bad thing? It would have saved countless supernatural creatures, so maybe not.

"It's time," one of the heroes standing guard by Haven's cell said.

The keys clanged when he opened the door. Haven stood tall. This was probably the last time he was making this walk, the last time he was going anywhere. It was his trial, and he would face it head on.

He wouldn't beg. He would *never* beg, not anyone but

Dimitri, nowhere but in bed with him.

He didn't protest when the heroes were too rough as they manhandled him toward the room in which the conclave met. He didn't say anything when they pushed him around, when the heroes gathered along the way stared at him, when they pointed at him, jeered, talked to each other. He didn't care what they thought. He was still convinced he'd done the right thing, and nothing would change his mind.

He swallowed when he arrived in front of the meeting room. This was it. It was the moment in which he'd be able to explain why he'd done what he'd done, and he could only hope the conclave would listen.

He didn't think they would.

The doors opened, and Haven was pushed inside. The heroes stayed outside, and Haven had to walk to the center of the room on his own.

He'd always thought the set up was a bit ridiculous. The conclave members were sitting on high benches set in a wide circle around the middle of the room so they were looking down at Haven. He supposed it was to make him feel like he was smaller than them and like he wasn't as good as they were, and it had worked for a long time. He'd only been here a few times, and never in this kind of situation. The other times, he'd obeyed their orders, and they'd been happy with him.

They weren't this time.

He stood there, waiting. He could feel the disapproving gazes on him, the anger floating in the room. They might not even ask questions. He wouldn't be surprised if that were the case and if they decided he should die right away.

"What do you have to say for yourself," a woman said.

Haven couldn't see who had spoken. The room was almost entirely dark, no doubt on purpose to scare and confuse him. Since he didn't know which way to turn, he stared right ahead. "I only have to say that I don't regret anything I did. I always believed what the conclave told me, and I took pride in being a hero, but I know better now."

"How dare you?" a man asked, but he stopped before explaining what he was talking about.

Haven waited a second.

Then, since no one else said anything, he continued. "The conclave, all of you, hate supernatural creatures whether or not they're criminals. You've been using your power and your authority over heroes, and you've used us as your weapons. Through us, you've managed to become even more powerful. Because *that's* what you're after. You don't really care about supernatural creatures, or about humanity. The only thing you care about is yourself, how much money you have, how much power. You've been using me and everyone else to get as much of it as you can, which is why you're going to kill me. You can't allow me to talk to anyone else, to make others realize what's going on. Why else wouldn't you even want to listen to a leshy who saves children?"

"He kills their parents," another man said.

"Do you know why he kills them? Have you ever bothered talking to him? I won't deny that Dimitri probably could have acted differently, but I saw one of those children. I saw what her father did to her, and honestly, I would have killed him myself if he hadn't already been dead. If it meant that man would never put his hands on his daughter again, I would have done much worse than tearing him apart, and it would have been my job as a hero."

"It's obvious he doesn't repent," the first woman said.

"Why should I repent? I already told you why I didn't kill Dimitri. We're not saving those children. That's our job, but we haven't been doing it. We are protectors of humanity, and instead of doing that, we've been killing people who would never hurt them."

"I've heard everything I needed to hear," said the first man, the one who'd been outraged by Haven's words.

Haven already knew what they would decide, and he wasn't surprised when the conclave condemned him to death in only a few minutes, with only one member against it. He almost expected it to happen right away in front of them, but of course, they wanted his death to be a message. They wanted the other heroes to see what would happen to them if they betrayed the conclave, and they would make a spectacle out of Haven's death.

That was why he'd been brought back to his cell. He didn't try to fight. He couldn't open a portal, since the cells were spelled to stop him from doing it. He had nowhere to go, no one who could help him. He was the only one who could save himself, and he knew he wouldn't be able to. He was going to die, and he was going to die soon.

When he entered his cell again, he made a beeline for the bench. If he only had a few hours left, he wanted to try to sleep and dream of Dimitri. He wanted one last good memory before he lost everything.

Dimitri jumped in his chair when Thor's cell phone rang. He tried to shrug it off, but everyone in the room knew how nervous he was. They didn't say anything about it, something for which he was grateful.

He couldn't stop thinking about Haven and what might be happening to him. He'd wanted to hope that Haven was right and that the conclave would take him back, and he hated that he'd been right. There was no going back for Haven, not the way he'd thought there would be. The only way forward when it came to the conclave was death, and that was what would happen to Haven if Dimitri didn't do anything.

He'd wanted to rush to help Haven, but Thor had managed

to convince him to wait. They needed more information. They needed to know what was happening and when it was going to happen, and they had to plan. They couldn't go into a conclave building without planning. It would be suicidal, something Dimitri wasn't.

He was willing to risk everything for Haven because he loved him, and because he wanted a future with him. He wouldn't allow the conclave to hurt either of them, and that meant he had to stop listening to his impulses and start listening to Thor, who apparently, was his conscience now.

"Yes?" Thor answered.

Once again, Dimitri didn't hear the other person on the phone, but Thor's expression told him everything he wanted to know. The conclave hadn't granted mercy to Haven. They were going to kill him, just like Dimitri had known they would.

"Thank you. I'll text you when we're close by. You don't have to do this, though. If we can manage to keep you with the heroes, it would be for the best. If you think they've discovered you, though, please, come away with us when it's time."

Thor's conversation lasted only seconds after that. He hung up, then looked around the kitchen table where they were all sitting. It was breakfast time, but no one was hungry. On the other hand, they'd already finished a pot of coffee.

"The conclave talked to Haven," Thor said.

"And?" Isaac asked. Dimitri could see he was hopeful. He was probably the only one in the room.

Thor shook his head. "They're going to execute him. Soon. *Today.* The only reason they haven't killed him yet is that they want to make an example out of him. They want every hero to see what happens to those who betray them. That's why they're organizing something big and public. We don't have much time to save him."

"But we have to go," Dimitri said, already getting to his feet.

Tryg grabbed his arm and pulled him back. "We'll help him," he snapped. Dimitri blinked at him, and Tryg's expression softened. "But you know we can't go in there without a plan. It's a conclave building. It's going to be crawling with heroes, especially with a public execution. We have to be extremely careful, and while Thor and I can probably pass for heroes, you absolutely can't. The horns are a dead giveaway, as are your hair and your beard."

"I'll shave everything off if it means I can go with you."

That startled a laugh out of Tryg. "I don't think that will be necessary, but I'll keep it in mind." He sobered up and looked at Thor. "What did you have in mind? I know you have blueprints of the place."

The corner of Thor's lips curled up. "Do I?"

"You're always prepared. You would have been a Boy Scout if they'd existed when we were human. Now talk. We don't have much time."

Thor nodded and grabbed his computer from the counter, almost falling off his chair. He opened it and clicked around, then turned it so everyone else at the table could see it. Sure enough, he had blueprints on the screen. "This is the building in which they're going to execute Haven. From what my informant told me, they chose this room," he said, tapping a fingertip on the screen. "It's where they have general meetings. It's the largest room, and we can't allow them to take Haven there. Like Tryg said, it'll be full of heroes and conclave members, and there are only two of us."

"Why two? I want to help," Cecil said.

Thor grimaced. "I know you want to, but the conclave—"

Cecil arched a brow. Thor snapped his mouth shut, and Cecil nodded at him. "I know you want to protect me. Trust me. I understand the feeling because I want to protect you, too. But I *can* help. I'm a mage, and I have magic powers neither you nor Tryg have. I'm not about to let the two of you go in without me. Besides, I'm sure Dimitri feels the same way."

Dimitri didn't have much power, but what he did have could help him to hide so he could reach Haven. If they planned this right, he could be useful. "I'm coming with you."

Isaac sighed heavily. "I already know I'm not coming, don't worry, Tryg. I'll be on the other side, checking the cameras." When he saw Dimitri looking at him, he grinned. "It's not the first time I've done this, and I'm more than able to help you from where I am."

Dimitri's throat felt tight. He wasn't alone. These people would help him rescue Haven. They cared about him, maybe not as much as Dimitri did, but they were still his friends, and they didn't want to see him die. Dimitri didn't know what he would have done if he hadn't had them. He didn't even want to think about it. He probably wouldn't have been able to save Haven, and then, Haven would have died. Instead, he had a fighting chance.

He swallowed. "What did you have in mind?" he asked Thor. He was the one with experience in this kind of thing, and he and Tryg would no doubt come up with a plan the four of them could follow. Dimitri didn't have the head for that, but he could follow orders, and he was planning on doing just that.

CHAPTER SEVENTEEN

Haven knew the time had come when the heroes came to take him out of his cell. He'd watched the evening fall through the tiny window, and he'd listened to the people talking in the hallway. They hadn't even tried to be discreet.

Haven already knew his execution was going to be as public as possible. It was the perfect way for the conclave to warn other heroes that they shouldn't step away from what they were supposed to do—obey the conclave without asking questions. If other heroes didn't want to end up like Haven, they would listen, and they wouldn't even think about whether or not the people they were sent to kill deserved it.

The news of why Haven was incarcerated and about to be killed was no doubt going around by now. There might be a few heroes who thought the way Haven did, but considering the situation, Haven doubted they would speak up. They knew better. If they didn't want to be executed right next to Haven, they had to keep their mouth shut, even if they knew that what was happening was wrong. Haven was only one hero. Saving him wouldn't help anyone but him, and at this point, everyone, including himself, knew it would be better and easier to let him die.

So this is it, he thought as the door opened. Two heroes stood there, staring at him. They weren't the ones who had dragged him around the building earlier, and they looked more serious, not as gleeful as the other two had been. They were probably older, and they understood what was going on better. Haven had no doubt he wasn't the only hero who'd thought about this kind of thing. He understood why no one had spoken up until now. He might not have if he hadn't fallen in love with Dimitri. But he had, and he couldn't kill Dimitri. He couldn't allow the conclave to hurt Dimitri, and he was going to pay for that. Hopefully, Thor and Tryg would make sure Dimitri was safe. They might not like Haven much, but Dimitri was different, and they'd make sure he was safe.

"Are you ready?" one of the heroes asked.

Haven shook his head. "Will I ever be ready to face something like this? I'm not ready to die, but I'm ready to go."

He suspected the conclave wasn't using heroes Haven knew so that there would be no chance of him escaping. They couldn't be a hundred percent sure Haven was the only one to think the way he did in the building. So instead of risking it, they'd had heroes come from other cities, heroes who wouldn't feel sorry for Haven, who wouldn't try to help him.

The three of them walked along the hallways. Haven was still handcuffed, and he didn't try to run. He had nowhere to run to, not when he couldn't even create a portal. Besides, he doubted the conclave would take the risk. They'd probably activated the spells that kept portals from being created in the building. It would have made sense, and even though Haven didn't respect the conclave, he couldn't deny they were smart. They knew what they were doing, and while some of them might be trying to do the right thing, the others only did this because they didn't want to lose everything—power, money, no doubt many other things they'd obtained by becoming conclave members. Haven had never thought about what it entailed, but clearly, he should have. He might have had more leverage on them if he had, but as it was, there was nothing more he could do about the situation.

They stopped in front of the wide room the conclave used when they wanted to talk to a big group. Haven had suspected this was where he would die, and he also had suspected Marsha would be waiting for him. She was there, in front of the closed door, her back ramrod straight.

Haven didn't want to talk to her, but he didn't think he had a choice. The heroes made him stop next to her, and together, they stood, waiting.

Marsha peered at Haven as if trying to read him. "I know what you think about me, but I never wanted this to happen," she said.

"Then you should have tried to stop it."

"I did. I told the conclave to give you another chance, but you already know their answer."

Haven hadn't been surprised by that. He'd already tested the conclave's authority with Thor. They wouldn't allow him to do it again for Dimitri or anyone else.

"Do you have anything else to tell me? Because I have an appointment," he said.

Marsha grimaced. "I wish you didn't feel that way toward me. I thought we were somewhat friends, Haven."

"Obviously we're not, since you betrayed me."

"I had to. It was the only way for me to try to save you. I knew you wouldn't hand over the leshy. You were clear about that. Trying to catch him was the only thing I could think of."

"But you didn't find him, did you?"

"I didn't. He wasn't in the forest, and you know it." She hesitated. "Why did you do it?"

"Because it was the right thing to do. You know that as well as I do."

"You could have tried changing the conclave from the inside. If you hadn't so spectacularly disobeyed their orders, they might have listened to you."

"But I would have had to kill Dimitri, and I couldn't. I've already killed too many innocent people. People who didn't deserve to die. I wasn't about to do that to him."

Haven had nothing to add. He turned away from Marsha

and toward the door, toward the conclave and the heroes waiting for him. He didn't think he'd ever be ready to face his death, so he supposed he was as ready as he could be.

Dimitri had never done anything like this, and he hoped he wasn't going to fuck it up. He wasn't used to rescue missions, not when it came to entering a place that was as well-guarded as the conclave building was. He saved children regularly, he supposed, but that was different. There was no one to protect them, to make sure he didn't get to them. There was no one ready to die in defense of them, and there surely was never anyone trained to hurt Dimitri in his attempt.

The heroes were.

Dimitri swallowed as he stared ahead. He could do this. He had to, for Haven. He couldn't allow Haven to get killed, not when there was something he could do.

It was dangerous. There was no denying that, and the four of them knew it. They hadn't talked about it, though. Dimitri knew he was mostly on his own. If anything happened, the other three would try to help him, but Thor would be focused on Cecil, and there was no way to know what Tryg would do. He might try to help Dimitri if he could, but he seemed to be in this more because he wanted to kick hero ass than because he wanted to rescue Haven.

Not that he didn't want that, of course. He wasn't crazy about Haven — Dimitri didn't have to ask to know that — but it didn't mean he wanted him to die. Still, the situation was precarious, and as Thor had said, the building was crawling with heroes. Dimitri hadn't realized so many of them would be there, and it made his stomach churn.

The conclave had organized a public execution, and everyone was here to watch it.

He didn't know how people could be that cruel. Why

would they want to watch someone die? Someone they'd fought with, someone who was technically their brother? Dimitri didn't understand, and he didn't want to. He didn't care how the heroes felt or why they felt that way. The only thing he cared about was Haven and getting him out of there.

"Ready?" Thor asked, looking at him.

Dimitri swallowed again and nodded. He *wasn't* ready. He didn't think he'd ever be because he didn't want to hurt people. He didn't usually, leaving that to his wolves. There would be no escaping it this time, though. If he wanted to save Haven, he'd have to get his hands dirty.

He had to swallow again because he felt like he was choking. "I'm ready," he confirmed.

Thor stared at him. "You don't have to come with us if you don't feel ready to do this. I understand, and I'm sure Haven will, too. This isn't something everyone can do. It won't be easy, and it won't be like anything you've ever had to go through before."

"I can do this. I have to. I love him, and I have to save him."

Thor stared at him for a moment longer, then, finally, he nodded and held out his hand. "Let's go, then."

Dimitri took Thor's offered hand while Cecil took the other. Dimitri's eyes widened when he turned them into smoke. Dimitri could shift, but it was nothing like this. It was incredible, and he looked down, amazed not to see his body. Unfortunately, he didn't have a lot of time to get used to it. Maybe it was a good thing. He didn't want to have too much time to think about what was happening and what he was about to do.

Tryg was ahead of them, and Dimitri saw him take material form behind the guards at the entrance. There were two of them, yet he took care of them without breaking a sweat. Dimitri was relieved he didn't have to do anything yet, but he knew that wouldn't last long.

Tryg moved to the side of the door, fiddling with the alarm system on the wall. From what Thor had been able to find out, the building was shielded against supernatural creatures who didn't wear special handcuffs the heroes put on them. That meant they couldn't go in, not until they disabled the security system. It was a good thing Tryg knew how to do that, and after a few moments, he looked up and nodded. Thor lowered them. Then, Tryg shifted again, and they moved inside the building.

Dimitri held his breath, but nothing happened. He'd expected to be swarmed by heroes, or at the very least, for some of them to notice them, but there was no one inside. Obviously, they thought that having two guards and a security system was enough to keep any undesirable guest outside. They should have known better, but Dimitri was grateful for the distraction, and for the fact that even if someone saw them, they wouldn't be able to touch them, not while they were still smoke.

It's probably best if we shift back, Thor murmured in Dimitri's mind, shocking him. *We won't be able to fight like this, and I doubt we can fool the heroes. They know what draugr can do.*

They'll notice us if we do, Cecil pointed out.

They'll notice us anyway. Dimitri, you could shift into a mouse. That way, you'll be less noticeable and safer.

Dimitri glared at him — or at least, he tried to, but he didn't have a face right now. *I already told you I don't care about my safety.*

Haven will, though.

Dimitri knew he was right, but there was no way he'd shift. He might not be a fighter like Thor and Tryg, but he wasn't useless.

Thor didn't ask again. They shifted back to human form, and Dimitri and Cecil let Thor and Tryg take the lead. They were used to this. It was their job, and Dimitri was more than happy to allow them to do it. Cecil did what he could with his magic, and Dimitri felt like the fourth wheel on a tricycle. He didn't have a reason to be here. He'd wanted to be because he wanted to help Haven, but he wasn't actually doing much except being nervous about having to kill someone. Maybe he should have stayed with Isaac, who was soothingly talking to them through the earbuds they all wore. He was telling them no one was waiting for them as they walked on, but Dimitri knew it wouldn't last long.

"Okay," Isaac said. "You have to turn to the right. That's where the room Thor told us about is." He hesitated. "People are standing outside, though. Four of them. I can't tell who they are, but one of them is wearing cuffs, and he was dragged there, so there's a good chance it's Haven."

Dimitri's heart raced. "Does he look okay?" he murmured.

"As far as I can tell. He's talking with a woman, but the two guards who brought him there are still hanging around. You don't have much time. You have to get to him before he's taken into that room. It's full of heroes, and when I say full, I mean it. There have to be at least fifty of them, maybe more."

And if they didn't reach Haven before he was taken inside, he would be executed. Isaac didn't have to say it. They'd already gone over it, and they knew they couldn't allow Haven to disappear into the room that was crawling with heroes even more so than the rest of the building.

Dimitri looked ahead. Thor peered back at him, nodded, then, together, the four of them turned the corner.

Haven wouldn't have been more surprised if his jaw really had hit the ground. It certainly felt like it as he watched Thor, Tryg, Cecil, and Dimitri stride down the hallway toward him.

He was the first to notice, but that didn't last long. One of the guards looked their way and reached for his sword.

Then all hell broke loose.

Everyone moved. One of the guards rushed toward the group coming for them while Marsha moved closer to Haven. The doors of the room he should have been executed in—and still might—slammed open, and a stream of heroes came out, ready to fight.

Haven and his friends wouldn't make it.

It just wasn't possible, not when there were only five of them, especially when two weren't trained to fight and one was handcuffed. They were going to get killed, and it was all because Haven had been an idiot and had ruined everything. He couldn't allow that to happen, and he tried to move forward, but his hands were still cuffed, and he wasn't going anywhere, not with the second guard still with him.

The guard pushed him against the wall, and Marsha came along, pressing her back next to Haven's. She looked around with wide eyes. People were already fighting, and to Haven's surprise, Dimitri was better at it than he'd expected.

Dimitri ducked as a sword came at his head, then, with one leg, he hit the hero and kicked him off balance. He was lucky the hero was one of the younger ones who weren't fully trained yet. He wouldn't have been able to do that otherwise.

It didn't take long for Haven to realize that Thor and Tryg were doing their best to take the oldest and more experienced heroes while leaving the others to Cecil and Dimitri. And while Cecil clearly wasn't used to physical fighting, he wasn't having too much of a problem as he used his magic as a weapon. He created barriers, pushed heroes away, knocked them off their feet, while Dimitri clubbed them upside the head with a sword he'd found. Instead of killing them, he was knocking them unconscious, and the sight made Haven's heart swell.

Dimitri didn't want to kill them. He only killed people who deserved it, and these heroes hadn't done anything but follow orders. They were blind, but eventually, Haven hoped they would see the truth and that they would hold the conclave accountable.

He wouldn't be there to see it.

Either way, whether he was killed or managed to escape, this was the last time he would be in this building.

A more experienced hero moved toward Dimitri, and when he turned his head, Haven realized it was Mather. He was healed by now, but it was obvious in his expression that he held a grudge. He raised his sword, grinning. Dimitri noticed him and took a step back, but he stumbled on the foot of one of the heroes on the floor, and he fell.

Haven tugged on his handcuffs. He had to save the man he loved. He couldn't, though, even though the guard who had been next to him was gone. He had to do something, but what?

He was considering throwing himself between Mather's sword and Dimitri when two hands on his made him look down.

Marsha was uncuffing him.

He snapped his head up to look at her. "What are you doing?"

"The right thing. Go help him. I can see you want to, and he and the others are your best bet to escape." She looked straight at Haven. "I never wanted you to die, but it doesn't mean I'm working against the conclave, so you have to go. I won't be able to do this a second time. Stay away from the conclave and live your life."

Haven hesitated, but in the end, he went. He didn't understand why Marsha had freed him, but he didn't think it mattered. Maybe she cared about him more than he'd thought. Maybe she believed she was doing the right thing even though she was going against conclave orders. Whatever the reason, he was free, and he could help Dimitri.

He threw himself against Mather's back, knocking him

down. Mather cried out, and his sword hit the floor. He rolled around to fight Haven, but Haven cocked his fist and clocked him on the face before he could do anything. It wasn't enough to put Mather down, though, and they rolled until Haven was on his back this time, Mather on top him. There was a glint in Mather's eyes that told Haven he wouldn't hesitate to kill him, so Haven wasn't surprised when Mather wrapped his hands around his neck.

He didn't have his sword anymore, so he was going to try to strangle Haven.

Strangling took a lot of strength, especially when it came to doing it to someone as big and strong as Haven. Haven knew he could get himself out of this eventually, but he didn't have to. A sword suddenly poked through Mather's chest. Mather looked down at it, incredulous, and his hold on Haven's neck slackened.

Haven pushed him away, rolled to his feet again, and looked at the person who had killed Mather with his own sword.

Dimitri.

Dimitri was staring down at Mather's body as if he couldn't believe what he'd done, and maybe he couldn't. As far as Haven knew, he'd never killed anyone. He usually left that to his wolves, and Haven wished he could have done that in this case, too. He didn't want Dimitri to have to kill anyone.

But he just had, and he'd done it for Haven.

Dimitri made a strangled sound and threw himself at Haven. Haven caught him, holding him close, wrapping his arms around him as he tried to soothe him. "I'm sorry you had to do that," he murmured, burying his face against Dimitri's neck.

Dimitri snorted. "You're sorry I had to do that? What are you talking about? I'm here to rescue you. You think I was going to watch him strangle you?"

Haven didn't tell him he could have freed himself. He

didn't want Dimitri to feel even worse about it. He moved closer and pressed their lips together. Dimitri's eyes widened, but he kissed him back, at least until someone hit them from the side. They almost fell, but Haven managed to keep them on their feet.

He found Tryg staring at them, obviously amused even though he was holding a bloody sword. "I don't think now is the right moment to do that, guys," he pointed out. Then, he grinned even wider and headed back into the mix, raising the sword he'd stolen from a hero.

Haven caught his arm before he could go far. "We'll never be able to kill all of them. We have to run."

Tryg nodded, then walked in Thor's direction, who was fighting and protecting Cecil. Together, they took care of the two heroes who were trying to take down Thor. Then, Thor grabbed Cecil's hand. Tryg got hold of Haven and Dimitri, and they were smoke.

Haven had known about this draugr power. He'd studied supernatural creatures most of his life, and he knew what draugr could do. It was stunning to be part of it, though. He knew his eyes would have been wide if he'd had them, but he didn't, even though he was looking down at the hallway in which they'd been fighting. The other heroes were running around, yelling, trying to get back to them, but they were too high.

They still had to leave. Sooner or later, the heroes would get their wits back and reactivate the security system someone had obviously disabled. Then Haven and the others would be stuck inside, unable to leave because they couldn't use their powers anymore.

Haven didn't know how to let Tryg know about it. He had no idea if he could communicate while they were smoke. But Thor and Tryg moved toward the exit, and as one, they traveled toward the front door.

It was close, but a group of heroes was standing in front of it.

Dammit. What now? Tryg asked. *We can try finding an open window, but it's going to take some time.*

Since he was speaking, Haven was pretty sure he could, too. *Go to the left,* he said.

You know what you're doing?

There's a room down the hallway there. We can sneak inside, and from there, I can open a portal.

There was a pause before the two clouds of smoke moved to the left.

Haven held his breath until they were in the room he mentioned. It wasn't big, just a closet used to stash brooms and cleaning supplies, and he doubted most heroes even knew it was there. He did, though, and he knew he could use it to open a portal even though it was a tight fit. The security system was down, but it wouldn't be for long, and he had to be quick.

He raised his hand in front of him as soon as he was back in his human form. He opened a portal the conclave couldn't track, then, as soon as it was open, looked at the others. "We have to go through, and we have to do it now. They're going to get the security system back up, and then, we'll be stuck here."

Thor dragged Cecil through the portal, then, Tryg went. That left Dimitri and Haven alone. Haven waited for Dimitri to step through the portal, but instead, Dimitri offered him his hand. Haven took it, and together, they left the conclave building.

Dimitri squeezed Haven's hand as they stepped through the portal. They walked into a forest, and Haven made a movement with his free hand, closing the portal behind them. They weren't out of the woods yet, though—both figuratively and literally.

Dimitri took a deep breath. He wanted to get the smell of sweat and blood out of his nose, but he felt like it would be stuck there forever. He'd killed a man, and he didn't know if he'd be able to deal with that. He would have to, though. He'd done it to save Haven, and he didn't regret it. He never would.

Haven looked at Thor. "Where to?"

"Paris. We can move as smoke once we're there and get to a safe place."

Cecil had managed to open a portal to get them to Haven, but it had taken a lot out of him, much more than it took out of Haven. It wasn't magic he often used, preferring to use human transportation, but they hadn't had time for that today.

By chance, Haven portaled them close to the Parisian apartment where Cecil, Isaac, Tryg, Thor, and Dimitri had been staying. Haven couldn't portal them closer because he'd never been there, but they got there fast enough, entering through the window they'd left open.

Cecil made a beeline for Isaac as soon as they were inside the house, and Tryg followed him. Thor, on the other hand, hung around for a second. He looked at Haven up and down. "We managed to get you in time."

"You did. I'm still in one piece." Haven turned so Dimitri and Thor could see he wasn't wounded. "Thank you."

Thor slapped Haven's back. "No need to thank us. You're one of us now. You're family."

He left then, going after the others, Haven staring at his back. Dimitri wasn't sure why, but he suspected it was the family part. It had surprised Dimitri, too. He'd known he was close to the four men now, but he'd thought they were doing this for him rather than to save Haven. Instead, it looked like they liked Haven as much as he did, albeit in a different way.

And now, he and Haven were alone.

Dimitri took a step back, dropping Haven's hand. He'd never felt so awkward, not even the first time they'd met, but he knew he had to do this. He didn't want Haven to be with him only because he'd been there to rescue him. He was in love with Haven, but he didn't know if Haven was in love with him. They'd never said the words. They hadn't had the chance to.

"We should talk," he murmured.

"Of course."

Dimitri looked around. He knew the others wouldn't come back. They no doubt realized he and Haven needed to talk, and they were giving them space. He was grateful, but on the other hand, it also made him uncomfortable. He still had no idea what to say. He supposed he should just get the words out.

He cleared his throat. "I know I was there to rescue you, and I don't regret it. I don't want you to be with me just because I helped you, though. The rescuing you doesn't have anything to do with our feelings. You can leave if you want. You can stay away from the conclave and from me, and I won't say anything."

Haven took a moment to answer, and when he did, he had a question. "You want me to leave, then?"

"Of course not." Dimitri swallowed and looked straight at Haven. "I never want you to leave. You shouldn't have left in the first place. It was stupid, and you almost died because of it."

"I already know I shouldn't have left. I regretted it as soon as I got there, but it was too late. You saved me, though. I'm sorry I put you through this. I never wanted to hurt you. I was just trying to do what was right, and now I know I went about it the wrong way."

Dimitri shook his head. "I understand why you did it. You don't have to atone for anything, though, Haven. I know you did some things you hate, but giving yourself up and dying won't solve anything. If you really want to help, you need to work toward that. You can help supernatural creatures in their fight against the heroes. You can work to get the conclave removed."

Haven cocked his head as if he couldn't quite believe what he was hearing. "Removed?"

"We'll talk about it later. I just wanted you to know that you don't have to be with me just because I saved you. That's all."

"What if I want to be with you because I love you?"

Dimitri sucked in a breath. He'd hoped, but he hadn't known for sure. "Do you? Love me, I mean?"

Haven stepped closer, taking one of Dimitri's hands again. "I do. I've loved you for a while, but I never told you because I thought we couldn't be together. Now I know we can. But I don't want you to be with me just because I'm back. Me being here doesn't mean we have to be together, although I would like us to be. I love you, Dimitri. I don't want to lose you, but if you'd rather take a step away from us, I'll understand. I hurt you, no matter what I was trying to do."

Dimitri rolled his eyes and threw his arms around Haven's neck. "You're going to have to work harder than that if you want to get rid of me. I'm not going anywhere. I love you, too, and we can do this — together."

He was relieved when Haven wrapped his arms around him and hugged him close. They stayed like that, holding each other for a while before Haven spoke against Dimitri's hair. "I'm sorry," he repeated.

Dimitri shook his head and buried his fingers into Haven's hair so he could tilt his head and look at him. "Don't be. I understand why you were clinging to the conclave and your work and worth as a hero. You don't know what you are now that you're not one anymore, but you don't see things the way

I do. You'll never stop being a hero, even if you don't work for the conclave. Like you told me, you were born a hero, and you'll die a hero. The fact that you're not working for the conclave anymore won't change that."

Haven moved away, looking at Dimitri. "I hope you're right. I have no idea what I'm going to do with my life now."

Dimitri cupped Haven's face with his hands and kissed him. "You don't have to worry about that now, but when you're ready, we'll figure it out together. I'm not going anywhere, Haven. I just got you back, and I fought hard to make that happen. I won't let anything come between us ever again."

For a second, Dimitri thought he'd gone too far, but Haven's smile reassured him. They kissed, and he knew everything would be okay.

They were in this together, and they would be in the future, too.

CHAPTER EIGHTEEN

When Haven woke up the day after Dimitri and the others had rescued him, he was still smiling. He felt like he would never stop, not when he would wake up in Dimitri's arms for years—hopefully, for the rest of his life. He didn't know anything else right now except for the fact that he was with Dimitri, and that was enough.

Dimitri turned to face him, dislodging Haven's arm from his waist. He gently cupped one of his cheeks. "You're feeling better," he commented.

"I am." It wasn't easy to come to terms with the fact that he was never going back, but Haven was starting to.

Seeing the way the heroes behaved, hearing what the conclave told him, helped. He couldn't change the conclave from the inside. He wasn't a conclave member, and they were too attached to their power to listen to a hero. They wouldn't give it up, and Haven was only one man. He hadn't been able to change the way they viewed supernatural creatures, but he hadn't given up yet. He would work to find a way to make at least the heroes see that what they were doing was no better than being professional killers, though. They weren't protecting humanity from supernatural creatures. They were protecting the conclave from them, and possibly themselves. It made no sense for them to go after supernatural creatures who lived their lives and those who helped human beings, yet, they did. That was all Haven needed to know.

He would always be a hero, just like Dimitri had told him yesterday, but he would be a hero in his own way. He couldn't go back, but that didn't mean he couldn't help humanity anyway. Hell, working with Dimitri would be enough to make that happen.

Haven wrapped his arms around Dimitri and pulled him close. "Everything isn't perfect, but I'll be fine," he said, kissing the side of Dimitri's neck.

Dimitri looked at him for a moment, then nodded. "All right. I'm going to believe you. But if you want to talk, you know you can come to me. I'll always be there for you. I love you."

That still amazed Haven, too. He hadn't been allowed to fall in love before, and it had been easy to resist, at least until he met Dimitri. Dimitri was such a gentle soul, yet he was also fierce when it came to the people he wanted to protect, and to Haven's awe, it included him. Dimitri loved him and wanted him in his life, and if there was one good thing about leaving the conclave and the heroes behind, it was that. Now that Haven was on his own, he wouldn't have to leave Dimitri's side.

Dimitri kissed him, and they almost lost themselves in each other. They would have if someone hadn't knocked on their door. "Are you awake?" Thor called out.

Haven groaned and rolled onto his back, hitting his head against his pillow. "What do you want? Will you go away if I say no?"

There was humor in Thor's voice when he answered. "Too late. I was just wondering if you were coming out for breakfast. It's ready."

Haven opened his mouth to say no, but Dimitri beat him to it. "We'll be right there. Give us five minutes."

"From the sounds coming from your room last night, you might want to shower," Thor pointed out.

Haven growled, grabbed his pillow, and threw it at the door, but he could already hear Thor walking away laughing.

"I hate him," he grumbled.

Dimitri kissed his cheek and untangled himself from the

sheets. "That's not true. You like him. He's your friend."

"Only because this is my life now. I don't have a choice." But they both knew that wasn't the truth. Even though Haven could have done without the teasing, he knew it meant Thor truly considered him a friend.

Haven had never had that. Even the heroes he'd been friendly with hadn't been friends. They hadn't been *allowed* to be friends. All of that was over now, though, and Haven kept that in mind as he and Dimitri quickly washed up and dressed.

He'd spent last night with Dimitri, and he suspected Thor and the others wanted to make sure he was fine. He was humbled by the way they cared about him, and he promised himself that from now on, they would be his priority. They and Dimitri were the only people who had cared about Haven and what happened to him. He couldn't ignore them. He didn't have to, now. They were his family, just like Thor had said yesterday, even though it was incredible to think that.

When they got to the kitchen, the other four men were already there, sitting at the table.

They weren't alone.

A blond man was sitting with them, sipping on a mug of coffee, and his gaze moved to Haven as soon as he heard him enter the room. There was something about him, a familiarity, but Haven didn't recognize him. He knew the man was safe, because otherwise, he wouldn't be in the house and Thor and Tryg wouldn't be so relaxed around him. He still made sure Dimitri stayed away from him, though, guiding him toward a chair on the other side of the table.

He could feel the man's gaze on him, tracking him around the kitchen as he filled two mugs with coffee and brought them to the table, which was laden with plates of food. There seemed to be everything on it, from pancakes to eggs and bacon, from fruit to French pastries.

"It's about time," Tryg muttered.

Isaac elbowed him in the ribs. "Shut up. You know they had to find their way back to each other."

"They did enough of that last night."

Isaac arched a brow. "I'm sorry, don't you remember how we were in the beginning?"

Tryg opened his mouth to say something, but he closed it again and shook his head. He hooked a hand behind Isaac's neck and pulled him closer, kissing him soundly and making him squeak.

Haven looked away, giving them some privacy, and his gaze caught the new guy's.

"Okay, so I know you've noticed him," Thor said. "Why don't you sit down? I'll introduce you."

"It's a bit hard not to notice him, since he's sitting at the table with us," Dimitri pointed out.

The man chuckled. "You're not wrong." He offered Dimitri his hand, and Dimitri had to lean over the table to shake it. "You're Dimitri, right?" the man asked.

"I am. I don't think I caught your name, though."

The man's smile widened. "That's because I didn't tell you. I'm Mordred."

Haven blinked. "I know someone with that name. Well, I've heard of him."

Mordred turned his attention back to Haven. "I'm pretty sure it's me you heard about. I was a hero for hundreds of years before I left the organization."

Haven clutched his mug. "Heroes don't leave the conclave."

"No? Isn't that what you just did?"

He was right. It *was* what Haven had just done, and it made sense. He'd heard of Mordred, but never that Mordred was dead — which he obviously wasn't. "What happened?" It was taboo to speak about him, and Haven had never asked questions. He wished he had now.

Mordred looked at Thor, who shrugged and looked at Haven. "Well, I thought you'd want to talk to Mordred. You're a hero, and now that you don't work for the conclave anymore, I know you're going to be at a loss at what to do. You want to protect humanity, and when you think about it, our jobs aren't that different. We kill bad guys."

Haven grimaced. "That's what I thought I was doing until recently. I killed the people the conclave wanted dead. I didn't ask questions, and I should have."

"And you know that now, which means that in the future, you'll focus on the bad guys. It's who you are, Haven. You might not work for the conclave anymore, but that doesn't make you less of a hero. Anyway, that's why I asked Mordred to come over. He's gone through what you went through, and he overcame it. I think we can all work together if you're okay with that, but again, you don't have to make any kind of decision right away. Take your time. Be with Dimitri. Enjoy being free. You have all the time in the world to make decisions when it comes to your future. You're immortal, and the conclave doesn't have a hold on you anymore."

Haven looked at Mordred. "Are you really only here because you want to talk about my future?"

Mordred's grin turned feral. "I am. I doubt you know about this, but after I left the conclave, I started my own organization of fallen heroes. Do you want to hear about it?"

It would be a kick in the balls to the conclave, and Haven found himself intrigued. He didn't know what he wanted his future to look like, but he had a choice, and he knew what he was good at. He knew he wanted the conclave to answer for their crimes, and he couldn't make that happen on his own.

He took Dimitri's hand under the table. He squeezed, and Dimitri squeezed back. "I'd like to hear about it, yes," he confirmed. Then, he listened.

YOU MAY ALSO ENJOY THE FOLLOWING FROM EXTASY BOOKS INC:

Valentine
Catherine Lievens

Excerpt

Val heard the front door slam. He couldn't help but smile. He'd thought the guy was cute when he'd first seen him, but now, he thought he was straight up adorable.

The guy had been talking to himself, something that endeared him to Val. It was obvious he hadn't realized someone was watching him, and Val was sorry that he had eventually. From the way he'd run inside, he'd been ashamed, and Val didn't want him to be. There was nothing to be ashamed of about falling down or even talking to yourself. Val did it sometimes, too.

He wasn't as cute and adorable as that guy had been when he did so, though.

He shook his head. No matter what he thought of the guy, he had to focus on the job. It was what he was being paid to do. He just was sorry that once he would be done, he wouldn't see the man again. Maybe he could try talking to him. He didn't want to scare him, but it could be worth a try. Not that he had to do it anytime soon. He and the others had been hired for several jobs around the property, and the roof was only the first step. It was the most important one, but there was plenty of work to do.

"Stop daydreaming," Niall said, but Val could hear the teasing in his voice.

"What, you can daydream and not work, and I can't?"

"That's because I'm the owner's nephew."

Val laughed. He knew Niall didn't mean anything by that. It was true his uncle owned the company they both worked for, but since he and Val had grown up together, the man might as well be Val's uncle, too.

However, he wouldn't be happy with either of them if he found out they weren't working, so Val did his best to focus on the work. They were right on time when it was time for them to pack up at the end of the day. They did so, and Val yearned for a shower, a cold beer, and something to fill his stomach.

"What will you be up to tonight?" Niall asked as he and Val climbed down the roof, following the others. Now that the work was over for the day, people were relaxing and talking. A few pride members had come out to offer the team refreshments, and Val looked around. He was hoping to catch a glimpse of the man he'd noticed, but he was nowhere to be seen.

Niall elbowed him in the ribs. "You're looking for him again."

"I am."

"You're not even going to deny it?"

"Why should I?"

Niall beamed. "No reason. You're just not this obvious with your crushes usually."

"I wouldn't call it a crush. I just think he's cute."

"And you wouldn't mind getting to know him better."

"I wouldn't, no." But he doubted the same could be said for the man. He'd run inside when he'd seen Val on the roof, although that might have been because Val had seen him fall.

Val would have no way to know, not until he talked to him. The guy wasn't here now, either, so maybe that was one more thing that pointed to him not being interested. Either that, or he was busy somewhere else.

Val was here at the pride to work, not to find himself a boyfriend. He couldn't help how cute he found the man, but he could stay away from him, at least for now. Maybe once the work was over, he could find him and ask him out. That way, he wouldn't be distracted while he worked, and he would give the guy time to get over whatever had happened today.

"Do you want some lemonade?" a man asked as he walked closer. He was holding a tray with sweating glasses, and the sight made Val realize how parched he was.

"Thank you," he said with a smile.

The man smiled back. "You're welcome. It's the least I can do since you didn't make us wait too long to repair the roof. Other companies wanted us to wait for months."

"That's because someone canceled a job," Niall said. He'd taken a glass, too, and he looked like he was enjoying it.

Val took a sip of his glass, and damn, it was good. "I'm Val," he introduced himself.

"Liam. I'm the alpha mate."

Val and Niall looked at each other. They were human, but they knew what an aloha mate was. "How should we address you?"

"As Liam. I wasn't always alpha mate, and I have to admit I'm not yet used to the role. Again, thank you for coming."

"Can I ask you a question?" Val said, the words crossing his lips before he could think about them.

Liam cocked his head. "Of course, although if it has to do with the roof or the house, you should probably ask my mate or Forest, the beta."

"It doesn't. I, well, I noticed a man earlier today. He went for a walk. Tallish, with messy brown hair."

Liam's smile told Val he suspected why Val was asking, but thankfully, he didn't ask. "That was probably Simon. He went for a walk earlier, after his job interview."

"Job interview?" Niall asked.

"For the alpha's personal assistant spot. He got it, and he probably needed to walk off the stress. He mentioned seeing someone on the roof when he came to Gal's office."

"Did he say anything else?" Val had to ask.

"No, but he was flustered." Liam hesitated. "You'll probably see him around the house once you start working inside. He's single as far as I know."

Niall guffawed. Val wasn't surprised Liam had seen right through him. "Thanks for the info."

"As long as you don't make me regret it."

"I hope I won't." Val couldn't make any promises, though. He couldn't read the future.

"How about we have dinner together?" Niall asked as they headed to Val's truck. They came to work together, even though Niall had his own car.

"I don't know. I really want to shower first."

Niall made a scene of waving his hand in front of his nose. "You need to. Maybe we can meet later?"

Val had been looking forward to flopping onto his couch and not move for the rest of the evening, but that didn't sound like a bad idea. He had to eat, after all, and he wasn't up for cooking. He also wasn't up for one of the frozen dinners in his freezer. "All right. Just give me time to shower, and I'll pick you up."

"Nah," Niall said, shaking his head. "I can drive to the pub. Don't worry about me. Just focus on your shower, and make it a long one. You really do need it."

Val reached out and slapped the back of Niall's head, even though he knew Niall was teasing. He didn't do it hard, and it made Niall laugh. Val ignored him and turned on the engine to drive out of the property.

"You really like that guy, don't you?" Niall asked after a while.

"I do."

"Why? You don't even know him. You never talked to him. You've only seen him from the roof, and it's not like Liam told you much about him."

"I don't know why. There's something about him, though. It made me want to climb off the roof and find him, ask him his name and if he wants to be with me."

Niall batted his lashes. "You think he would throw himself in your arms?"

"Very funny. What about you? No one's caught your eye lately?"

"No one who belongs to the pride, no. Besides, you know me. I'm not looking for a relationship the way you are. I'm a free man."

"Sure you are." Val suspected it was more because Niall hadn't found the right person yet than because he was against it, but he didn't ask.

Niall wasn't wrong. Between the two of them, he was the one who had more one-night stands and boyfriends who stayed with him for only a few weeks, a month at the most. Val didn't even bother with one-night stands, not anymore. He'd had his fill of them when he was younger, and now, just like Niall had said, he wanted a relationship. He wanted to settle down, to have a home, to have someone to go back to every evening. He didn't like having an empty house, but so far, that was the only thing he had, and he would have to make do.

"And you really don't care that he's a shifter?" Niall asked, his voice more serious now.

"Why should I care?"

"I don't know. I'm not saying you should, but plenty of people would."

"Would you? If he was a guy you're interested in?"

"Hell, no. I'm pretty sure I fucked a few shifters here and there over the years. But we don't know anything about the pride. We don't know what happened in there."

"Then we'll find out."

"It's as easy as that, is it?"

Val wasn't sure it would be. There had to be a good reason for which the pride had stayed away from the town for all these years, and he wanted to find out what it was. He was wary of asking Simon out until he did. Maybe it was nothing, or maybe it was. Maybe there was something wrong with all the shifters in the pride.

But no. Val couldn't think like that. They were shifters, yes, but that didn't make them any different from the other shifters in town, or even from Val and Niall, even though they were human. The Green Hill pride was made up of human beings, people who were trying to open up, to become part of Green Hill. They wanted to be part of the community, and it was a good thing. Val couldn't start thinking they were dangerous without even knowing what had happened in the past. He had to think of them as individuals, not as a group in which everyone was the same.

Because they weren't the same. Simon was the cutest guy Val had ever seen, and he was planning on finding out whether or not they could work as a couple.

Nothing that had happened in the past would change that.

ABOUT THE AUTHOR

Catherine is the creator of several series, most of them paranormal, including the Whitedell Pride Series and the Gillham Pack Series. While she graduated in translation, she decided to go the writer's way because it was more fun to create her own stories and characters.

She's been living in Italy for more than twenty years, but she's a daughter of the North—Belgium to be precise—and she misses it so much that she's already planning to move back.

She loves pizza—probably too much—her son, her pets, and of course, books. She sneaks some reading time into her schedule every time she has five minutes free from writing, demands from her various pets and son, and lastly, housework.

Connect with her:

lievens.catherine@gmail.com
BookBub: https://www.bookbub.com/authors/catherine-lievens
Website: https://authorcatherinelievens.com/
Facebook: https://www.facebook.com/catherine.lievens.9
Facebook Group: https://www.facebook.com/groups/411788002341528/
Twitter: https://twitter.com/authorCLievens
Newsletter: http://eepurl.com/c-uvKn

www.ingramcontent.com/pod-product-compliance
Lightning Source LLC
Chambersburg PA
CBHW070837120626
46556CB00002B/783